The woman was screaming,

trying desperately to escape her attackers.

Chas noticed absently that she was tall and slender, with pale blond hair. Very nice. But completely beside the point.

Who she was, what she looked like, was unimportant. For now. She needed help, and if she didn't get it soon, she was going to stop being a person and turn into a statistic. Chas frowned. He would just as soon avoid that.

"Okay, boys," he announced. "Fun's over. Let her go."

The men looked startled at his silent approach. One of them pulled a knife.

Bad idea.

From the dockside dives in Hong Kong to smugglers' dens in the mountains of Nepal, there was no shortage of people who could have explained that going after Chas Howell was just not something you wanted to do.

Ever.

Dear Reader,

Welcome to another month of top-notch reading from Silhouette Intimate Moments. Our American Hero title this month is called *Keeper,* and you can bet this book will be one of *your* keepers. Written by one of your favorite authors, Patricia Gardner Evans, it's a book that will involve you from the first page and refuse to let you go until you've finished every word.

Our Romantic Traditions miniseries is still going strong. This month's offering, Carla Cassidy's *Try To Remember,* is an amnesia story—but you won't forget it once you're done! The rest of the month features gems by Maura Seger, Laura Parker (back at Silhouette after a too-long absence), Rebecca Daniels and new author Laurie Walker. I think you'll enjoy them all.

And in months to come, you can expect more equally wonderful books by more equally wonderful authors— including Dallas Schulze and Rachel Lee. Here at Silhouette Intimate Moments, the loving just gets better and better every month.

Happy reading!

Leslie Wainger
Senior Editor and Editorial Coordinator

Please address questions and book requests to:
Reader Service
U.S.: P.O. Box 1325, Buffalo, NY 14269
Canadian: P.O. Box 1050, Niagara Falls, Ont. L2E 7G7

FULL OF SURPRISES

Maura Seger

Silhouette®

INTIMATE MOMENTS®

Published by Silhouette Books

America's Publisher of Contemporary Romance

SILHOUETTE BOOKS

ISBN 0-373-07561-8

FULL OF SURPRISES

Books by Maura Seger

Silhouette Intimate Moments

Silver Zephyr #61
Golden Chimera #96
Comes a Stranger #108
Shadows of the Heart #137
Quest of the Eagle #149
Dark of the Moon #162
Happily Ever After #176
Legacy #194
Sea Gate #209
Day and Night #224
Conflict of Interest #236
Unforgettable #253
Change of Plans #280
Painted Lady #342
Caught in the Act #389
Sir Flynn and Lady Constance #404
Castle of Dreams #464
Man of the Hour #492
Prince Conor #520
Full of Surprises #561

Silhouette Desire

Cajun Summer #282
Treasure Hunt #295
Princess McGee #723

Silhouette Special Edition

A Gift Beyond Price #135

Silhouette Books

Silhouette Christmas Stories 1986
"Starbright"

MAURA SEGER

and her husband, Michael, met while they were both working for the same company. Married after a whirlwind courtship that might have been taken directly from a romance novel, Maura credits her husband's patient support and good humor for helping her fulfill the lifelong dream of being a writer.

Currently writing contemporaries for Silhouette and historicals for Harlequin and mainstream, she finds that writing each book is an adventure filled with fascinating people who never fail to surprise her.

Chapter 1

The white line down the middle of the road seemed to heave up in the glare of the headlights and ripple a good couple of feet above the highway. Chas Howell blinked hard and automatically shifted his foot to the brake.

He was alone in the darkness, not having seen another car in at least half an hour, but he wasn't inclined to take chances. Nodding off at the wheel was one of the stupidest ways he could think of to go.

Truth be told, there'd been a time when he wouldn't have cared. That he did now, quite fiercely, filled him with bone-deep gratitude. He'd screwed up enough in his life to regard second chances as nothing short of miraculous. Having gotten his hands on one, he wasn't about to throw it away.

Rolling down the windows, he breathed in the cool, sage-scented air of the New Mexico night. It felt good on his face, blowing the cobwebs away and sending the small, twisted things that sometimes clawed at him back down deep into their caves.

A mile or so up the road there was a glow on the horizon, that silent, silvered announcement that human beings are present. Chas headed for it. Gradually he made out a low, salmon-colored building surrounded by a parking lot. A neon sign above the doors showed a cowboy endlessly twirling a lasso and the words Pecos Bar and Grill.

If he'd hit Pecos, he was farther than he'd thought. But then, he'd obviously lost track of time back there on the endless highway, driving through the night with only his own thoughts for company. Pulling into the parking lot, he killed the engine and sat for a minute, rubbing the kinks out of the back of his neck.

It was then that he heard the scream.

He paused, hand frozen on the back of his neck, and listened. The parking lot wasn't well lit. With his headlights turned off, he could see little. Maybe he'd heard wrong. All he wanted was a quiet burger and a beer. No trouble. There had been plenty of that in recent years, he didn't need any more.

The wind was blowing pretty strong. It could play tricks with a man's hearing. For just a moment he thought that might be what was happening, but then the screams started again, louder now and coming one right after another. They were real.

Worse yet, they belonged to a woman. She sounded caught between stark terror and fierce anger, with terror having the edge.

Chas sighed. He dropped his hand, opened the door and got out of the car. The doors to the bar were shut and the music bouncing against the walls would keep anyone inside from hearing. There was no one else in the parking lot except him and the woman and—

Two big guys wearing checked shirts and jeans, with lots of hair. They were unshaven, more beefy than muscular, but strong enough for what they had in mind. One had his arm around the woman's waist, trying to shove her through the passenger door of a pickup truck. The other was trying to get hold of her legs but she kept kicking out, holding him off as best she could.

The second guy had to keep dodging her, but the first one had a firm hold and he was winning. Another minute or two and she'd be inside that truck. Where she definitely did not seem to want to go.

Chas shook his head in disgust. He was very careful not to let himself think too much about the evil that seemed to inflict so much of the world, because when he did think about it he tended to get very, very angry. But there were times when there was just no avoiding it.

He walked more quickly toward the truck, stride lengthening, arms flexing slightly, his long, lean body seemingly relaxed. The impression was deceptive but not entirely so. He was completely in control and utterly calm.

The Turk had called him a killing machine, but then the Turk loved melodrama. The fact was he never killed—unless he had to. And he absolutely never enjoyed it. Much.

The woman was still screaming, trying desperately to get away. He noticed absently that she was tall and slender, with pale blond hair that looked like spun taffy. Very nice, but completely beside the point.

Who she was, what she looked like, was unimportant. She needed help and if she didn't get it soon, she was going to stop being a person and turn into a statistic. He'd just as soon avoid that.

He stopped a few yards from the truck, stuck his thumbs in his belt loops and smiled. "Okay, boys, fun's over. Put her down."

The men turned. They looked startled but unimpressed. The one holding her laughed. He muttered an obscenity.

Chas frowned. He turned to the woman. "Just so we're all on the same track here, do you want to go with these men?"

Her eyes widened. They were large and thickly fringed. He stared into them, momentarily distracted. Deep within them, past all the fear and shock, he thought he glimpsed a well of calm determination mingled with keen intelligence. But he could easily have been mistaken.

"No," she said. Her voice rasped, roughened by all that screaming.

"Okay," he said and smiled.

"What're you, crazy?" the second man demanded. He pulled a knife from his back pocket and flipped it open. "I'm gonna cut you bad 'less you get away from here right now."

His friend grinned, revealing an urgent need for dental work. "Hurt him, Charlie. Go ahead."

Charlie nodded. He moved away from the woman and advanced on Chas. Bad idea, very bad, as any number of men scattered over much of the world could have told him.

From dockside dives in Hong Kong to smugglers' dens in the mountains of Nepal, there was no shortage of people who could have explained that going after Chas Howell was just not something you wanted to do. Ever. But none of them happened to be there in the parking lot of the Pecos Bar and Grill.

Which, Chas decided, was just as well. If he'd ever seen two good old boys in need of one of life's tougher lessons, these were them.

He moved, or more precisely, he flowed into the night, through it and around, a whisper of sound on the air, a flash of blinding speed and relentless strength. Charlie fell, writhing in agony, lacking breath to scream.

The first man shouted something and threw the woman to the ground. He launched himself at Chas. It was over in seconds. He, too, lay—arms wrapped around his middle—twisting in blinding pain.

The woman picked herself up. In the dim light of the parking lot, she looked very pale. Her hair tumbled around her shoulders like a nimbus he'd seen once surrounding the moon in the South Pacific. He blinked again, feeling suddenly as though he were

back on the road, staring at something he hadn't expected to see.

"How did you do that?" she asked huskily.

He shrugged, bent down and picked up first one
man, then the other, tossing them both into the cab of
the pickup. "Just lucky, I guess." He banged hard
against the door, making both men cringe. "Go on
now. Get out of here."

They complied, just barely. The pickup went slowly
out of the lot, stopped, started up again more quickly
and vanished into the night. Chas was left alone with
the woman.

"You all right?"

"Oh, yeah, peachy. This is just how I like to spend
my evenings." Her voice shook slightly, but her expression was defiant. It softened as she continued to
stare at him. "Look, I really owe you. If you hadn't
come along—"

"Forget it," he said quickly. "Do you have a car
here?"

She nodded. "Over there."

"I'll say good-night, then." He didn't wear a hat so
he couldn't tip it. Besides, he would have felt a little
foolish doing that. But he did incline his head politely
before he turned away and headed after what he'd
come for in the first place, a semidecent meal.

Annalise Johannsen stared after him, dumb-
founded. Her legs felt like jelly, her stomach was doing flip-flops and she was completely shaken by the
thoroughly unpleasant sensation of surprise at simply

being alive and safe, two conditions she'd hitherto taken pretty much for granted.

She'd seen it happen—heck, she'd been center stage. But, aside from television, she'd never witnessed anything like what he'd done, and she still wasn't sure what had really happened.

However, the goons were gone—that much she did know—and she was still in one piece. Score one for the good guys.

She brushed herself off, trying to ignore how much her hands shook, and did a quick check for damage, still thinking about her rescuer. She didn't even know his name. He'd gone before she could ask him.

In fact, she'd barely had a chance to say thanks. If she didn't know better, she'd have thought she imagined him. Only the lingering soreness where she'd hit the ground hard on her backside told her it had been all too real. If Mr. Tall, Lean and Ruthless hadn't shown up when he had, she'd be in that pickup right now.

The thought made her skin crawl and caused her to take several deep breaths, fast. She was a brave woman, but there were limits to what anybody could expect to tolerate. Going one-on-one, or more correctly, two-on-one, with the goon boys wasn't high on her list.

A slight smile curved her full mouth, surprising her as much as it would have anybody who happened to see it. Bad though this was, and worse though it could have been, there was a small ray of sunshine.

She'd bet just about anything she had that the goons were hurting real bad. It had all happened so fast, she couldn't be sure, but she thought she'd heard at least a couple of bones crack. They'd be hurting even worse tomorrow, and it would be a long time, if ever, before they forgot what had come at them.

Which brought up a point: Where, exactly, had her rescuer come from? She glanced around the parking lot. There were maybe a dozen cars and trucks, typical for a Wednesday night at the Pecos. Later, when the music really got going, there'd be a few more, and on Saturdays the place was packed.

But now she could pretty much recognize everyone who was there. All except that car at the end, the one with the busted front fender and the piece of trim coming off the passenger door. That one.

Was that his? That wreck? It didn't look like it could go more than a mile or two, so how had he gotten it here, dead center in the back of beyond with the nearest city a hundred miles in either direction and nothing but ranches and badlands in between?

She walked around it slowly, Partly to get a good look and partly because her legs still weren't steady enough for anything fast. It was a four-door light green Volkswagen, a model the company hadn't made since the early 1980s. Solid chassis, well constructed, unusually good engine. She'd known a guy at college who had had one and she'd done a tune-up for him once. It was a workhorse car—nothing flashy, but dependable.

The interior was in good shape and neat. No suitcases to be seen, no coffee cups, fast food bags or maps. Nothing to give any clue to the car's owner.

Time was, you didn't see foreign cars in a place like Pecos. But these days people were filtering through from the West Coast and back East, bringing all sorts of things with them. Still, nobody local—which meant a radius of roughly five hundred miles—would drive anything like this.

She went around the front and peered more closely at the busted fender. There was rust where the metal was split. It had happened a while ago then and he hadn't gotten it repaired. No money?

She hadn't noticed much about what he was wearing, but she seemed to recall washed khakis and a blue cambric work shirt. No fringed shirt or beaded vest favored by some of the boys who patronized the Pecos. Ditto on the hand-tooled boots and the leather chaps. If he had money, he sure wasn't showing it. Not on himself or on his car.

Slowly Annalise straightened and stared off in the direction the pickup had gone. Her stomach was settling down and the sheer, skin-itching horror was passing. Still, she couldn't fool herself. She'd been lucky this time. There was nothing to say she would be again. If there was one lesson she'd learned over the years, it was to trust her instincts. And they were telling her just one thing.

She turned, straightened her shoulders and headed into the bar.

Chapter 2

Chas slid into a booth toward the back. The music wasn't quite as loud there and the smoke was a little less thick. Most of the other patrons were clustered together near the front, around the big-screen TV, within easy reach of the complimentary ribs.

He stretched out and closed his eyes. He'd driven four hundred miles since dawn, over a thousand in the past few days. But it was worth it. He'd had two really great weeks with Jimmy, camping out, fishing— the works. A smile flashed across his mouth at the memory.

"Get you something, honey?"

Chas opened his eyes. The waitress was maybe nineteen, with hot-combed hair, a wad of chewing gum and jeans that looked sprayed on. She ran her eyes over him blatantly.

"A burger," he said, "medium, side of fries and whatever you've got on draft."

"Sure thing, honey." She wiggled off, but came back almost immediately with the beer. Setting it on the table, she dipped low enough to give him a passably good view of cleavage that was somewhere between healthy and downright robust. "Anything else you'd like?" she asked.

"How about a salad?"

She cracked her gum, tossed her hair and went off. Chas sipped his beer. She was a good-looking girl, but therein lay the problem. He'd given up girls a long time ago. It was women he liked.

The one in the parking lot, for instance. She was maybe twenty-eight, could be thirty. Only a few inches shorter than him, which put her at about five-nine. Slender, with that sun-drenched hair and those grayish green eyes that had a touch of topaz. Eyes he wouldn't be likely to forget.

She had courage, too. Not much in the way of self-defense training, but she'd sure tried. The screams had been smart, the only way she'd had to attract help. But she hadn't panicked. There'd been no sign of hysteria in her. She'd picked herself up and looked him straight in the eye.

Just like she was looking at him right now, walking down the length of the bar, a slight, unconscious sway to her hips and a set to her head that told him here was trouble.

She stopped, looked down at him and said softly, "Buy you a drink?"

Chas gestured to the beer, hiding his surprise. He honestly hadn't expected to see her again. "I've already got one."

"Good for you." She slid into the booth opposite him, sat back and gave him a long, steady look. "I wanted to say thanks."

"You did that already."

"It bears repeating."

Whatever else, she didn't discourage easily. Nobody coming across her would guess what she'd been through just a few minutes before. Her oval-shaped face was slightly flushed, her lips full and ripe, and she smiled easily all the way to her eyes. She looked relaxed, confident and just plain nice.

He was a cautious man by nature and experience. But he also had a natural helping of curiosity, especially when it came to a woman like this. "My name's Chas Howell," he said. "What's yours?"

"Annalise Johannsen. I really am very grateful to you, Mr. Howell."

"Chas. Care to join me?"

She had dimples at the corners of her mouth. "I thought I already had."

"For a burger, or have you already eaten?"

"No, I haven't. Sounds good."

The waitress returned, saw Annalise and frowned. "Get you something?"

"What he's having. Put it on my tab." She made a small gesture that took in his dinner.

Chas's brows, as golden brown as his hair, rose slightly. He'd met a whole lot of people in his life, but he couldn't remember any of them being a pretty woman quite like this one. A woman with a genuine smile who ran a tab in a place like Pecos.

"It's the least I can do. So, are you just passing through?"

"Maybe. You from around here?"

She nodded. "I've got a place outside of town."

I've got. Not *My husband and I,* or *My family.* Just *I.* He glanced at her hand. No ring. She had an independent air about her that suggested there had never been one.

"Just out of curiosity, did you know those two guys?"

Annalise shook her head. "No, but I think I've seen them around once or twice." The waitress brought her beer. She took a sip and eyed him over the rim. "What kind of work do you do?"

"This and that." He gestured to his burger. "Want half of this till yours comes?"

"Yeah, sure."

He split the burger in two and passed her half on a napkin, along with a handful of fries. They ate in silence for a few minutes.

"More of this or more of that?" she asked.

"Depends. What kind of place do you have?"

"I raise horses."

"Oh, yeah? I've done some horse training."

"Where?"

"Down in Argentina. Been doing it long?"

"Most of my life. Listen, I could use some help, and if you're not too busy with this and that right now, maybe you could use a job. What do you say?"

"No, thanks. Catsup?"

"Not so fast. You said you were passing through. Are you in a hurry to get somewhere?"

"Not particularly."

"I pay well. Three square meals a day, a roof over your head and four hundred bucks a week. What do you say?"

"I'd say you must have the happiest horse hands around."

"I've run the place by myself, at least up until now."

"What's changed?" Before she could reply, he answered the question himself. "The goons in the parking lot."

Annalise nodded. "That's right."

"They just spook you, or is there something else?"

"Something else. I need somebody around for at least the next few weeks until I can get a few things straightened out."

Chas put the burger down and looked at her straight. "Lady, if you're thinking you need protection, why not go to the cops?"

"No crime's been committed, unless you count what happened out in the parking lot, and they won't. Look, chances are, this will be the end of it. I just want to be extra sure, that's all. You get a place to stay and some money in your pocket. What's the harm?"

The corners of his mouth twitched. He particularly liked the money angle. She must figure he really needed it.

"Four hundred a week?"

"That's right."

"Well, I'm sorry, I'd like to help out, but I think it would really be better for both of us if you went to the law. There's no sense taking chances."

"Five hundred. But I can't afford more than that."

"It's not the money, honest. I'm just not much good staying put anyplace. And besides, like I said, if there's really a problem, you need to talk to the cops."

"You won't reconsider?"

He shook his head. "Sorry."

Annalise stood up. "No harm done."

"What about your order?"

"You have it. I'm not hungry anymore. Thanks again for your help."

"Yeah, sure."

She was gone so quickly, he wasn't sure she'd heard him. He sat for a while, but his appetite was pretty much gone, too. When he got tired of thinking about wide places in the road and nights full of surprises, he signaled for the check.

Chapter 3

She was going to regret this in the morning. Decent, law-abiding people didn't behave this way. But he was perfect, absolutely perfect, and she was really doing him a favor. Look at the car, look at the clothes. He was too proud to accept her help even when he more than deserved it.

Okay, as rationales went, it wasn't the best. But it was all she had. Bottom line, she needed help and Chas Howell fit the bill to a T. And with just a little more time, she was sure she could convince him of that.

Nice engine, looked as though it had been pressure cleaned more than once. He might drive what appeared to be a wreck, but he kept what was under the hood in tip-top condition. Which made her feel all the guiltier. One little thump with the hammer—that was all it would take. She could manage that much.

Done. Quick as the long-eared hares who made their burrows beyond her paddocks, she slammed the hood down and headed back to her own car. There she settled down to wait.

It didn't take long. Not twenty minutes after she'd left the Pecos, Chas Howell did the same. He paused for a moment right outside the doors, giving her a good opportunity to assess him once again. Yep, he was just the way he'd seemed inside—long, lean, hard, and more good-looking than any man had a right to be. But also with a tough edge to him, a solitariness that piqued her curiosity. She'd have to watch that. She wanted protection, not more trouble. On that score, she already had plenty.

He strolled over to the car, an innately graceful man, got in and put the key in the ignition. Annalise held her breath. She really did feel bad.

Nothing happened. Through the windshield, she could see him frown and try again. Nothing.

He got out, went around the front and propped the hood up. Annalise eased her foot off the brake and let her car roll forward. By the time Chas straightened up, scowling, she had pulled up next to him.

"Trouble?" she asked, giving him a bright smile.

"Battery case is cracked."

"Is that bad?" Was her nose growing?

"Bad enough. Is there a service station around here?"

"Oh, sure, no problem. You want Mickey's, about ten miles south. Of course, he isn't there now."

"Who usually gets called if there's an emergency?"

"If somebody goes up in a fireball, the state police. Otherwise, folks figure it can wait till tomorrow."

"Great," Chas muttered. "I don't suppose there's a motel."

"'Fraid not."

He gave her a long, assessing look that reached right down to her toes and curled them. "Got a spare bed?"

Her smile widened. "Hop in."

Chas settled back in the passenger seat, propped his elbow on the open window and stared out at the night. Annalise Johannsen drove fast but well. But then he was getting the impression that she was like that in a lot of things.

She looked so damn innocent, sitting there, fingers curled lightly around the steering wheel, hair blowing in the breeze. Why did he have the feeling he was being had?

Coincidences happened. The battery was a year old and had seen hard use. He'd had it in the back of his mind that it ought to be replaced. It could have simply cracked.

But if it had, it sure suited Annalise's convenience. He was right where she'd wanted him, if only temporarily.

"I'll be out of here tomorrow," he said, reminding her and himself, as well. It was a good idea to remember that, sitting there with the light perfume she wore floating on every breath he took and the brightness of her smile warming him clear through. Definitely to-morrow.

"Fine," she murmured. "Whatever you say."

In a pig's eye, Chas thought. Miss Annalise Johannsen was a lot of things, but sweetly agreeable wasn't on the list. No doubt about it, she looked real pleased with herself.

"You know much about cars?" he asked, just in passing.

"I can keep one going." She was hedging; he was sure of it. But he had nothing to pin her down on and besides, the fact was he wasn't going anywhere before morning. He'd slept in a back seat often enough to know he didn't want to do it again. That spare bed of hers was the best option he had.

She turned off the main road and headed up a dirt track toward a light in the distance. Soon enough, Chas spotted a house. It was a two-story, white clapboard with a porch out front. There was nothing fancy about it, but the rosebushes around the steps and the curtains in the windows added a homey touch.

"The bunkhouse is around back," Annalise said as they got out of the car. "I'll find you some sheets and blankets."

Chas nodded. She walked on ahead of him. He followed. As she climbed the steps, her jeans molded over her bottom, revealing the high, firm curve. A bolt of desire went through him. The intensity of it shocked him. He was a highly controlled man, so long accustomed to keeping his needs and emotions in check that he was hardly aware of doing so. Yet now, in the back of beyond with night closing in, he suddenly had to suppress the instinct to reach out and touch Annalise.

His hands curled into fists. He stayed behind in the hallway as she went to get the linens. More to distract himself than from any particular interest, he glanced around. Beyond the hall, he caught a glimpse of a living room and on the other side, what appeared to be an office. Both looked clean, comfortably furnished and inviting. There were braided rugs on the polished floors, overstuffed furniture, a scattering of plants, not much in the way of clutter. Rooms to stretch out and relax in after a long day.

He was reminded of Jimmy's home, the cheerful, sun-washed rooms, the sense of warmth and welcome. This house was much the same. Hard on the desire he had felt came a sense of longing as intense in its own way as any sexual hunger could be. He closed his eyes against it, willing it to dissolve, and was rewarded when it faded, leaving only a faint residue of wishfulness.

Annalise came back down the stairs. She was carrying a pile of sheets, blankets, towels and pillows. "If you'll take these, I'll get a lantern."

Chas obliged. Together, they went back outside and around the far end of the house. A short distance away was a long, low building and beyond that were the stables.

"I hope you'll be comfortable," she said as she opened the bunkhouse door and stood aside for him to enter. "This hasn't been used in a while but it should be all right."

"Looks fine," he assured her, taking a quick glance around. A table and chairs were positioned around a potbellied stove. Nearby were two rows of bunk beds, enough to sleep a dozen men. "This must have been a pretty big spread at one time."

"It still is," Annalise said, "but these days, I rent out most of the land and just keep what I need for the horses."

He nodded. It made sense. A woman running a place on her own might not like the idea of needing a dozen men around to keep it going.

"The bathroom's through there," she said, gesturing toward a door. "If there's nothing else—"

"This is fine," he assured her. "Thanks."

"Breakfast is at six."

"What time does the service station open?"

"About eight. I'll run you over there whenever you like."

She was being very accommodating. Another minute or two, he might be tempted to see exactly how far that would extend. Annoyed at his own susceptibility, he nodded curtly. "Good night."

As she turned to leave, a gust of wind blew in through the door. It caught her hair and sent it swirling around her head like a pale golden cloud. At the same time, her clothes flattened against her, exposing every slender, perfectly formed curve.

"Weather's changing," she murmured.

In all sorts of ways, Chas thought, and shut the door behind her.

Chapter 4

Annalise walked back to the house quickly. The wind blowing hard against her back urged her along, but mostly it was pure instinct that kept her going until she was upstairs in her own room, the curtains pulled and the bedside light illuminating a safe, familiar scene.

There was nothing remotely safe about Chas Howell—or familiar. She had quite simply never met anyone like him. No man had ever had the effect he had on her.

As she turned on the shower and let the water heat up, she told herself there was an obvious explanation for the attraction she felt. He had come into her life like Sir Galahad riding to the rescue, saved her from the goons and sent her senses swimming with a combination of rugged masculinity and old-fashioned protectiveness. Wrap all that up in a flat-out gorgeous package of long limbs, hard muscles and drop-dead smile and it was no wonder her insides felt like jelly.

She'd be fine. A nice hot shower, a good night's sleep and come morning, she'd be back to her old self. Chas Howell was hired help, nothing more. Of course, he didn't realize that yet, but he would soon enough.

Standing under the water, she made a mental note to call Jimmy O'Hare down at the garage real early. That done, her mind drifted to thoughts about what had happened in the parking lot. And what had almost happened.

She shivered slightly despite the hot water. Try though she might, she couldn't convince herself that it had just been a random attack. She'd gotten out of her car, and started toward the Pecos, seeing the two men in the shadows off to the side. Something in the way they'd stood, not casually, but purposefully, had put her on alert. She had already been speeding up, ready to make a run for the door, when they'd grabbed her. Just as they had, she was sure she'd seen a look of recognition on their faces, as though they hadn't been waiting for just any woman but her in particular.

Maybe she was wrong. It had all happened so fast, and the terror had been so great, that she could be misinterpreting. But the suspicion that it might have been deliberate lingered as she dried off and dropped a nightie over her head.

A few minutes later, lying in bed, she listened to the sounds filtering in through the window and tried hard to relax. Inevitably, her thoughts drifted to her guest and how he was doing out in the bunkhouse.

Just fine, no doubt. He gave every evidence of being a lone wolf, one of those intrinsically self-possessed men expert at looking after themselves with no need or use for the comforts a woman might offer beyond the strictly obvious. Exactly what the situation called for.

Tomorrow she'd call O'Hare, then she'd have to level with Chas Howell. That wouldn't be pretty, but she'd get through it, just like she had everything else. She'd be okay—she had to be.

The rain that had been coming on for several hours started at last. It pitter-pattered lightly against the sides of the house and filled the air with the smell of moist earth. She snuggled down under the covers, her eyes growing heavy until finally they fluttered shut.

Chas lay on his back, arms folded beneath his head, and stared up at the ceiling of the bunkhouse. The bed was surprisingly comfortable and the surroundings could hardly have been more peaceful. He should have been asleep, not thinking about a certain pale-haired woman with the light of challenge in her eyes.

The more he thought about Annalise, the more convinced he became that his being there was no accident. She'd said she needed someone around for a couple of weeks until she could get a few things straightened out. What things? Straightened out how? And why didn't she think the cops would pay any attention if she went to them for help?

The more he considered the situation, the less he liked it. If she really was in trouble, he didn't much feel like walking away. On the other hand, what could he, realistically, do? For all that some people might think otherwise, he was no hired gun. He was just an ordinary man, who, for his own reasons, preferred to be left to himself—except for Jimmy, of course. Better she realize that she needed a different solution to her problem—whatever it might be.

He'd tell her that again in the morning before he left. If she absolutely couldn't see her way clear, he would give her a few phone numbers. There were people he knew who would do the work she wanted. He could get someone out here, have it looked into, make sure she was really okay before he—

Chas shook his head wryly. He barely knew the woman and already he was trying to decide how to sort out her life so that he could walk away with a clear conscience. He'd be smarter to remember that she was a grown-up in her own right who was clearly more than able to make decisions for herself.

Still, maybe he'd just give her those phone numbers.

The rain was getting heavier. He lay there, stretched out full length, and listened to it hitting against the roof. It was a peaceful sound, the kind that was sure to lull him into sleep. And it would have, except for the sudden plop of water against his face.

One plop, another, then another. He opened his eyes and scowled up at the ceiling. A bead of water formed, swelled and fell—straight onto his nose.

Chas muttered a mild curse. He'd slept in too many out-of-the-way places to be put out by a little leak. It was simple enough to just move to another bed.

He pulled the covers off and walked halfway down the length of the bunkhouse before picking another bed. Five minutes later, he was just starting to drift off again when—*plop*.

This time, the curse was a little less mild. He got up again, headed for another bed, but took a careful look at the section of the roof above. Even as he watched, it began to leak.

She'd told him the bunkhouse hadn't been used in a while and she hadn't been kidding. If there'd been no alternative, he would have managed. But he was tired after the long drive and in no mood to get rained on all night.

Bare chested, wearing only khakis and boots, with a blanket tossed over one shoulder, Chas strode back out into the night. Moments later, he was banging hard on Annalise's door.

Chapter 5

"I'm terribly sorry," Annalise said. She'd bolted from bed at the sound of the knocking, grabbed a robe and run downstairs. Still half-asleep, she was trying to come to grips with the implacably masculine apparition standing smack-dab in front of her.

It wasn't easy. Bare chested, hair rumpled, with drops of rain clinging to his absurdly long eyelashes, Chas Howell was enough to knock any woman off her heels. Annalise was no exception.

Clearing her throat, she said, "I had no idea. The bunkhouse has been empty for almost three years and I've only gone in there to sweep every once in a while."

"No problem," Chas said. He took one quick, all-encompassing glance at her and looked away. "Point me to a couch and I'll be fine."

"Actually, there's a spare bedroom. You'll be more comfortable there." She was embarrassed not to have offered it to him before, instead of the bunkhouse. It was a sign of how much he made her aware of herself as a woman.

"Great." He stood waiting, still not looking at her, a tired, disheveled, glorious male who had the disconcerting effect of making her feel like a green girl, except that even back when she was a girl, she hadn't felt like this. The closest she could get to it was a near-death experience she'd had on a roller coaster, but she wasn't going to think about that just now.

"This way," she said, and was not at all surprised when her voice shook slightly. Mercifully, he didn't seem to notice. She led the way to the small room on the first floor at the back of the house. The bed was already made up.

He nodded curtly, a clear dismissal, and waited for her to leave.

"Good night," she murmured as she fled with as much dignity as she could muster. Back upstairs, lying in her own bed, she thought sleep must surely prove impossible. But somehow the knowledge that Chas Howell was under her very roof, so close that she could almost hear the creaking of the bedstead when he turned, made her feel oddly comforted.

The next thing she knew, it was almost dawn. The rain had stopped and the day looked washed clean. She rose and dressed quickly, her thoughts exactly where they had been when sleep claimed her—on him.

In jeans and a plaid shirt, with her hair in a ponytail and only cold water and good intentions on her face, she went downstairs to the kitchen. Remorse weighed heavily upon her. After all she had put him through—and what she was about to inflict—the least she could do was fix him a decent breakfast.

But first a quick phone call.

Jimmy O'Hare was the soul of understanding, especially considering the fact that she'd roused him from his bed to get her message. That done, she put the coffee on and set herself to making pancakes.

Something was burning. The smell dragged Chas out of deep sleep and sent him bolt upright in bed. His first thought was that the house was on fire. He was already reaching for his boots when he realized it wasn't quite that bad, just close to it.

Following the stink, he made his way to the kitchen. Annalise was there—why didn't that surprise him?— running water into a pan she held with one hand while with the other she pushed a window farther open.

"Problem?" he asked.

She whirled, and dropped the pan. It missed her foot by maybe an inch. They stared at each other.

Last night she'd looked exquisitely feminine in that frothy white robe she'd been wearing, with her hair tumbling around her shoulders. Now she was all practicality, in jeans and a ponytail, but she was still staggeringly beautiful.

Which was the real woman? The frightened but valiant almost-victim in the parking lot? The forthright would-be employer? The seeming helping hand who just might have helped him into being stranded? Frothy femininity, or ponytailed practicality? Whichever she was, whatever combination, there was one thing for certain—she sure as hell couldn't cook.

"What was this?" he asked as he bent and picked up the charred pan.

"Breakfast." She shrugged apologetically. "I must have turned the fire up a little too high. No problem. I'll just start over."

She sounded as if she were used to having to do this. He set the pan back in the sink and ran a hand through his hair distractedly. "Yeah, well, I'm sort of hungry and I'd like to actually eat this morning, so how about I just take care of it?"

Her eyes widened. "You can cook?"

"I manage. I'll tell you what. You go feed the horses and I'll fix something for the humans—okay?"

She hesitated. "Gee, I don't know. You're a guest after all, and it doesn't seem right asking you to do the cooking."

Chas glanced at the pan again, took in the chaos on the counter and squared his shoulders. "I insist."

"If you're really sure . . ."

"The sooner you get going, the sooner we eat."

She went, but not without a backward glance that made him realize he wasn't really dressed for company. Ten minutes went for a quick shower, a shave and fresh clothes. That done, he tackled the kitchen.

Half an hour later, he stuck his head out the back door and called Annalise.

Bliss, absolute, total bliss. Orange juice, pancakes that were golden, not burned, big dollops of slowly melting butter, and maple syrup that had actually been warmed. All that plus real coffee, not the slush she usually ended up with.

"You really can cook," she marveled as she stared at the wonders in front of her. Not the least of them was Chas himself, no longer sleepy and disheveled, but crisp, calm and completely in control.

Which didn't describe her at all, not if the flutter in her stomach and the flush creeping over her cheeks were anything to go by. She took a quick sip of coffee and dug in hungrily.

They ate in silence for several minutes. The pancakes melted on her tongue, the orange juice—which she knew to be frozen—conspired to taste fresh squeezed, and the coffee— She shut her eyes in pure pleasure.

"Where did you learn to do this?" she asked when she'd opened them again.

He shrugged. "Here and there."

"Is that kind of like this and that?"

His smile was sudden, male and toe tingling. "Very similar. Now I understand what you were doing at the Pecos last night—trying to get something decent to eat."

"It's true," she admitted. "I keep hoping a fast-food place will open up around here but so far no luck."

He grimaced. "Those places can kill you. Cooking isn't hard."

"If you say so." She was unconvinced. "What else have you done?"

His smile vanished. He shot her a quick, hard look. "What do you mean?"

Uh-oh, hit a nerve there. He definitely had something he didn't want to talk about. Dampening her curiosity, if only temporarily, she said, "Besides cooking, horse training and chasing off bad guys."

He relaxed again and refilled both their cups. "I was an acrobat for a while."

"You're kidding!"

"Nope. I was traveling in the Ural Mountains and I met up with an acrobatic troupe. They invited me to join them. It was a great way to see the country."

"The Urals . . . they're in Russia."

"That's right."

"You were an acrobat in Russia?"

He nodded. "I had somebody I was supposed to meet back in the States—we were going camping—so I couldn't stay long, but it was great while it lasted."

"This may sound like a stupid question, but what were you doing in the Urals to begin with?"

"I'd been in Siberia and decided to head back that way."

"Oh, well that makes perfect sense. Everybody I know in Siberia stops off to do acrobatics in the Urals before going camping."

Chas laughed. He had the grace to look abashed. "I guess you could say I've bummed around a lot."

"No, you couldn't. Guys who try to hitch rides on the interstate late at night are bumming around. You were adventuring."

His eyes crinkled up. He looked amused. "Is that a word?"

"It must be. Nothing else suits you."

His gaze met hers. The pancakes—sinful though they were—were momentarily forgotten. Sunlight streamed in through the windows. That must be what was causing the dazzled, warmed-from-within feeling spiraling through her.

"I ought to call the service station," Chas said.

She blinked once, twice, as though coming out of a dream. "I guess you'd better." As he got up, she kept her eyes focused on her plate. What was left of the pancakes still looked delicious, but she wasn't hungry anymore.

He found the number in the slim book hanging by a string beside the phone and punched it in. Annalise pushed the pieces around on her plate and did her best not to listen.

Chapter 6

"That's funny," Chas said. He didn't sound amused.

Annalise glanced up, the picture of innocence. "What is?"

"O'Hare, down at the service station, says he's real sorry but he can't fix the battery before Monday. Seems he doesn't have any in stock, has to send for one, the weekend's coming, he's got to go fishing, and so on."

He sat down again at the kitchen table, his legs stretched out in front of him, and eyed her closely. "I've been a lot of places, but this is the first time I've found a mechanic who needed four days to replace a battery. Hell, I got it done in three in a place that wasn't on any map I ever found and where people spoke a language I'd never even heard of."

"Jimmy's not what you could call real industrious."

"Obviously. What are the odds I can convince you to drive me someplace where I can get a battery for myself?"

"Gee, I'd love to, but I've got this problem to deal with and—"

"And I'm going to be stuck here whether I want to or not. Okay, let's have it."

"Have what?"

"The truth. As long as I'm here anyway, you might as well tell me why you were trying to hire me."

She took a quick breath. "Does that mean you're interested in the job?"

"It means I've got nothing else to do for the next four days and I'd just as soon know why. The cracked battery case I might be able to buy, but the bozo mechanic is just stretching it too far. There has to be a good reason why you'd jump through hoops to keep me here." Ominously, he added, "Or at least there damn well better be."

For a split second, he thought she was going to deny it. But then she sighed deeply, her shoulders sagging. "I'm sorry. I really feel guilty, but you need a job and I need help, so I figured there wasn't any real harm in getting you to hang around for a while. I was wrong. If I'd thought it out longer, or if I hadn't been so scared last night in the parking lot, I would have realized that."

Annalise stood up. "I'll call Jimmy. He'll get your car fixed today. I'll pay for it, of course." She started for the phone.

Chas stared at her back. Either she was even smarter than he figured or she really was sorry. Maybe both. A long sigh escaped him. All he'd wanted was a burger and beer. It looked as though he was going to get a whole lot more.

"Wait a minute."

She paused, hand on the receiver. "What is it?"

"Sit down."

"I can still catch Jimmy before he goes fishing."

"I said, 'Sit down.'"

She sat. He stared at the wall for a minute, telling himself he was crazy to even consider helping her. She'd vandalized his car, lied to him and deliberately tried to trap him in a situation in which he'd said he didn't want to be. Yet she had courage and strength. And she made him feel more alive than he had in a very long time. He felt compelled to at least hear her out.

"Tell me," he said, and sat back to listen.

"His name is Brad Fuller." Annalise's voice was very low. She sat with her hands cupping the coffee mug, her gaze focused on the slowly curling steam. "He owns a spread a few miles down the road. But according to him, he's the rightful owner of this one, too."

"Is he?" Chas asked.

She shook her head firmly. "No way. This land's been in my family for four generations. I inherited from my uncle when he died three years ago. Everybody expected that and nobody was surprised by it. But now, suddenly, Fuller's come up with what he claims is a document giving him the land."

"On what basis?"

"He says he loaned my uncle money shortly before his death on the condition that if it wasn't repaid, he'd take title to the ranch."

"Did you know anything about a loan?"

"Absolutely not. Besides, if my uncle had needed money, Brad Fuller's the last person he would have gone to."

"Not one of nature's noblemen?"

Annalise shook her head. "More like something that crawled out from under a rock."

"Has he offered any proof that the loan existed?"

"He says he's got a document and he's willing to take it into court. But he also offered me a settlement—fifty thousand dollars in return for my walking away."

Chas frowned. "That doesn't make any sense. He says he already owns the ranch but he'll still pay you for it?"

"He claims to want to avoid the hassle of suing me." Her mouth tightened. "Also, he wants to be nice."

"And in return, you be nice to him?"

"Something like that. Anyway, I told him to forget it."

"Which he hasn't?"

She hesitated. "I'm not sure. That was a few weeks ago. He got angry—real angry—and told me I'd regret it, but that was the last I heard . . . maybe."

"Maybe?"

"There have been a couple of problems. The owners of several horses I'm supposed to start training called and bowed out. That can happen, but three at the same time is unusual. Then some of the fencing was knocked down. I spent a couple of days rounding up ponies that had strayed and fixing the posts." She paused a moment. "Then my truck got firebombed."

Chas sat up a little straighter. "Your *what* got *what?*"

"I can't actually prove an explosive was used, but the truck was just sitting in the driveway one night, and there was this big boom and it wasn't there anymore. Just pieces of it."

"When was this?"

"Three nights ago."

"Dare I ask what happened when you reported it to the sheriff?"

"He said he'd heard there was a problem with that model."

Chas's face tightened. He'd been around far too much not to understand that there was corruption and violence everywhere. But that didn't mean he had to like it.

"Why didn't you tell me this last night?"

"And have you hightail it?"

"Oh, I see. You figured you'd bring me home, show me I could be living in the lap of luxury out in the bunkhouse, fix me a gourmet breakfast and I'd fold?"

She flushed slightly. "Okay, it was a dumb plan, but don't forget the five hundred dollars a week. That still stands."

It was a lot to her, he was sure. But it was meaningless to him. Still, he wasn't entirely without an incentive. Deep down he hated seeing anyone get away with this kind of thing. Plus his curiosity was piqued. What did Brad Fuller really hope to gain?

"Do you have any idea who those guys were last night?" he asked.

"I can't give you any names but I've seen them around. They work for Fuller."

Chas nodded slowly. He stood and started picking up the dishes.

"What are you doing?" Annalise asked.

"Cleaning up. Then we're going to take a ride into town. I want you to show me around."

She gave him a quick, shy smile. "You don't have to do this."

"I know."

"There's no way I can really thank you."

His eyes ran over her slowly. She was a damn good-looking woman, the kind that would wear well on a man should he ever be disposed to hang around long enough to find out. Which, he reminded himself, he definitely wasn't. Still there was no law to say he couldn't enjoy looking at her. He watched the flush creep over her cheeks and smiled. "Yeah, you can."

"How?" she asked, just a little huskily.

"You dry," he said, and tossed her the towel.

Chapter 7

Chas drove. Annalise sat and looked out the window. It was kind of nice for a change to just relax, let somebody else do the work. Let somebody else be in charge.

For a change. She didn't think she was likely to get used to it but for a few weeks, she'd manage. Meanwhile, she smiled as she considered what the reaction would be when they got into town.

"This is it," she said as the road widened and rows of buildings materialized on either side. "If you blink, you miss it."

"It's livelier than a lot of towns in these parts. Any parts, come to think of it."

Annalise nodded. It was true. Pecos had been luckier than a lot of other wide-spot-in-the-road towns. "They used to run cattle through here, then there was a brief thing with oil. Now it's ranching mainly, the occasional tourist and a meat-processing plant that's fortunately another five miles or so down the road."

"What brings the tourists?"

Annalise gestured in the direction of the hills rising out of the desert beyond the town. "There were Anasazi here once. You can still see what's left of their settlement. It's a lot smaller than some of the others that have been found, but there's enough for people to come by and take a look."

"I wouldn't mind doing that myself," Chas said. "I worked for a while on a dig down in southern Mexico. It was fascinating."

"That was before the acrobats?"

He grinned. "And after the four months on a fishing trawler. Aside from a job I had once in a sugar-refining plant in Jamaica, the fishing trawler was definitely the worst."

"Is there anything you *haven't* done?"

He cast her a quick, impenetrable look. "Lots of things. Held a steady job, for one. Played bodyguard, for another."

"Don't think of it that way. You're strictly for appearances."

His eyebrows rose. "I am?"

"Sure. The way I see it, by now Fuller knows all about what happened in the parking lot last night. Better yet, so do all the guys who work for him. With you hanging around, he's going to have an awful hard time convincing anyone to take another try at me."

"You think so? Has it occurred to you that he might just send *more* men the next time? Or that they might be a whole lot better armed?"

She paled slightly. "I'm betting that he isn't totally nuts."

"This isn't poker. It just might be your life that's on the table."

"So what do you suggest? That I turn tail and run?"

He sighed. "Would it do any good?"

"No, this is my land and this is where I stay."

"I figured. Okay, when we get out of this car, you follow my lead. Whatever I do, you go along. Understood?"

"I guess so...."

"No guessing. You agree or the deal's off."

She hesitated, but only barely. There was no real choice and besides, she instinctively trusted Chas. It was a shock to realize how much.

"All right," she said quietly. He slipped the car into a parking spot and got out. She followed.

Chas pulled a pair of sunglasses from his shirt pocket, put them on and stood looking up and down the street. "This way," he said and headed for a storefront on the other side.

The girl behind the counter blinked hard. She looked up from the form Chas had just handed her, glanced from him to Annalise and back again. Peggy Sue Wilson was all of twenty years old and didn't have a wrinkle to call her own. But she'd gotten her forehead scrunched up so hard, it looked like it would stay that way forever.

"That will be twenty-one dollars and forty cents, sir."

Chas took out a brown leather wallet from his back pocket and paid her. With the sunglasses on, his eyes gave away nothing. Gruffly he asked, "When will he get it?"

Peggy Sue blinked again. "It will go out immediately, sir."

Chas nodded. "Good." He turned and took Annalise's arm in a gesture that was blatantly proprietary. "Let's go."

Well aware that Peggy Sue was just about falling off her stool staring at them, Annalise kept her mouth shut and went along. But once outside, she could contain herself no longer. "What was that all about?"

"That? That was step one—sending a little message to a friend of mine."

"By telegraph?"

"Sure, why not?"

"You could have just called."

"Yeah, but if I had, that young lady in there wouldn't have anything to tell her friends."

There was a sinking feeling in Annalise's stomach. "What exactly did the message say?"

"Told a guy I know that I'm down here helping out a lady friend and to stand by with a few of the guys in case there's more trouble than I want to handle alone."

"Wait a minute. I can't afford to hire any more people."

"I know that. This friend of mine is over in the Middle East right now. The message will land on his answering machine. I'll leave another message telling him to disregard it."

"Won't he think that's strange?"

Chas considered for a moment. He shook his head. "Don't see why he should."

Maybe it would be better not to dwell too much on the fact that he had friends who wouldn't find such communications odd. "What else did you tell him?" she asked instead, suspecting she wasn't going to like this answer much better, either.

Chas looked pleased with himself. "To get some of the stuff I left with him ready to go. I tacked on a regular laundry list, bunch of semiautomatic weapons, a whole lot of ammo, some explosives. You name it, I put it on. Except, of course, for all the stuff I told him I already had with me, just so he wouldn't bother hauling it down, too."

They'd reached the other side of the street. Annalise dug her heels in. Reluctantly, Chas stopped, but he kept his hand on her arm. "What's the matter?"

"You're not telling me that you left guns, ammunition, whatever, in your car overnight while it was sitting at the Pecos?"

He grinned down at her. "I left a lacrosse stick, a bag of laundry I haven't gotten around to doing yet and a translation of the *Odyssey*. The point is, that nice young lady just had the most exciting telegram she's ever seen come across her counter. She knows she isn't supposed to reveal its contents to anyone, but what do you want to bet, this is one time she'll make an exception?''

Understanding dawned. Softly Annalise said, ''And it'll get back to Fuller?''

''How long do you think it will take? Half an hour, hour?''

''Are you kidding? Fifteen minutes, tops.''

He smiled. ''Good, that gives us time for step two.''

The Pecos was closed, but the Shamrock Café was doing a brisk business. They found a booth near the door. Annalise sat down first. Chas slipped in next to her and sat close enough that their thighs brushed. She stiffened a little in surprise, but he merely looked at her blandly and propped his arm along the back of the seat so that it was almost, but not quite, touching her.

The waitress came over. ''Hey, Annalise,'' she said, looking at Chas. ''How you doing this morning?''

''Just fine, thanks, Liz. I'll have coffee, please.''

''And for you?'' Liz asked, giving Chas a long, slow once-over.

He took off his sunglasses, put them in his shirt pocket and crinkled up his eyes. ''Coffee for me, too.''

Liz went away, but not without a backward glance. Chas sat for a moment before he spotted a cigarette machine off to the side.

''Excuse me,'' he said, standing. His hand brushed the back of Annalise's hair. Before she had time to think, he bent and touched his mouth lightly to hers. ''Be right back.''

He ambled off with a lean-hipped, lazy stride that made her blood heat. Aware that her cheeks were warm, Annalise looked away hastily.

Liz chuckled softly. Setting down the coffee cups, she said, "Nice going, honey."

It was on the tip of Annalise's tongue to deny there was anything between her and Chas but then she remembered her promise to him. She kept silent as Liz walked away, watching as he returned. When he had slid into the booth beside her, she said, "I didn't know you smoked."

"I don't."

Her eyes widened. Was everything he did calculated even to the extent of staging a small scene that made it look as though they might be lovers?

"You?" he asked.

She shook her head. "My only vice is chocolate ice cream."

He laughed, a low, supremely masculine sound. "You ought to think about broadening your horizons."

She looked away, confused by her feelings. Chas sat back and sipped his coffee. From the corner of her eye, Annalise saw several people glance their way. It was all too easy to guess what they were thinking.

Ruefully, she admitted that Chas had to get top marks for misdirection. Step one told Fuller he was no longer after just a lone woman, but was in danger of confronting a heavily armed contingent. Step two suggested why.

"I'm almost afraid to ask," she murmured, "but I've got to know. What's step three?"

"That depends on Fuller."

Annalise glanced toward the door. Her back stiffened. "In that case, it looks as though we're about to find out."

Chapter 8

Brad Fuller blew into the Shamrock Café resplendent in one of his trademark gray silk suits—handmade by this great little guy over in Hong Kong. He had on his Stetson—handmade by this great little guy over in Tucson—and his thousand-dollar boots—handmade by this great little guy over in Santa Fe. Sticking out of his mouth was his killer cigar—handmade by these really terrific folks down in Brazil. His oversize Caddy was parked out front, long horns on the fender. He was a big man with sharp brown eyes, a broad smile and a backslapping manner that served him well, as Brad himself was the first to say, in a statehouse or a bawdy house—didn't matter which.

"Miz Annalise," he said, brushing the rim of his hat with his thumb. "How you doing this fine mornin'?"

She fished up a smile from somewhere deep down inside and came right back. "I'm doing great, Brad. How're you doing?"

"Can't complain. Hell, nobody'd listen if I did. Who's your friend?"

Chas had been sitting back, quietly watching Fuller. Now he stood, unfolding to his full six-foot-plus length, long and hard, unsmiling. "Chas Howell," he said.

The two men shook hands. Annalise thought it might turn into one of those macho things, each trying to cripple the other for life. But they merely eyed each other warily and let it go.

"Well, now," Fuller said as he slid into the booth, "we don't get too many visitors here in Pecos, 'cept of course for folks who like to snoop around where those Injuns used to live. What brings you here?"

Chas sat down, leaned back, legs stuck out to the side, and shrugged. "Like you said, I'm a friend of Annalise's." He said her name real slow and gentle, dragging out the syllables like a caress. When he finished, he smiled just a little.

"Oh, yeah," Fuller said, man-to-man, as though she wasn't even sitting there. "Well, that's fine. Known each other long?"

"Long enough," Chas said.

"You're not from around here, are you?"

"I'm from a lot of places."

"Seems like. Couple of my boys came back last night pretty beat-up. They say you done it."

"That a fact?"

"Yeah, it is. And little Peggy Sue over at the telegraph, she claims you're armed to the teeth and sending for reinforcements." Fuller's eyes narrowed, turning hard as flint. "What you planning here, boy, some kind of war?"

Chas laughed. He made it sound like that was the best joke he'd heard in a long time. Looking perfectly pleasant, as though he actually thought Fuller was a great guy, he said, "Since when can't a man do a little target shooting? You got some kind of law against that?"

"You didn't say nothing about that. You said doing a job for a lady friend."

Chas looked surprised. "Didn't Annalise tell you? She's got a terrible problem with snakes out at her place. They're all over. Why, one of them crawled into her truck the other night and blew it to kingdom come. Can you imagine?"

Fuller's face reddened. He sat there, filling up the opposite side of the booth, a big, mean, angry presence. "I can imagine a lot of things, starting with some smart-ass stranger sticking his head in where it's gonna get shot off. Wouldn't want that to happen, would we?"

"Sure wouldn't," Chas agreed.

"Then maybe the smart thing for you to do is convince your friend here to sell out to me and the two of you vamoose."

"Can I get in here?" Annalise began.

"No," both men said simultaneously.

"The way I see it," Chas went on, ignoring her glare, "you ought to take the lady's word for it when she says she's not selling. If you really believe the land's yours, go through the courts. Hell, you might even win."

"He can't win," Annalise said. "There's no way my uncle ever—"

"I don't have time for that crap," Fuller said. "I bent over backward to make her a fair offer and what thanks did I get? Sooner she wises up and gets out, the better for everybody." He looked hard at Chas. "And that includes you, smart boy, 'less you want to find yourself in the fight of your life."

You could have heard a pin drop in the café. Nobody was even pretending to be doing anything except listening to what was happening. Liz stood frozen behind the counter. Sammy Roscoe, who ran the place, had come out from the kitchen so he could hear better, and a couple of guys from the meat-packing plant were leaning so far off their stools, they were defying gravity.

Fuller stood. He hitched up his pants, stuck his cigar back in his mouth and glared. "You remember what I said. I'm a patient man, but there's limits."

Chas didn't move. Unlike everyone else in the café, he looked perfectly at ease. "There's something you ought to keep in mind, too," he said.

"What's that?" Fuller demanded.

"I'm just a drifter, and Annalise can pick up someplace else if she has to. The stakes aren't as high for us." He stood up, slowly, his face suddenly so grim that Annalise herself flinched. It was as though a hot desert wind, heavy with the smell of lightning, had suddenly blown in, warning of terrible things to come.

Fuller sensed it, too. He remained frozen in place, staring at Chas as if he'd just that second seen him for the first time.

"But you," Chas went on, "you've got a whole lot more to lose. Your whole life, everything that makes it worth living, depends on never crossing paths with the likes of me, because I don't give a damn about how much money or power you think you have." He bared his teeth in what no one, not even the most innocent, would have taken for a smile. "Call it friendly advice, but before you raise a hand to this woman again, you think long and hard about what I'll do to you."

Fuller opened his mouth, closed it, opened it again. He looked like a fish flopped up on the side of the dock, out of his element. Annalise held her breath, sure he was going to say or do something. But he only threw one final look of raw hatred at Chas and slammed out of the café.

In the silence that followed, only one person spoke.

"Whoo-ee," Liz said. "Never thought I'd see that in all my born days." She patted her coiffure, sniffed loudly and hoisted the coffeepot. "Now who's ready for a refill?"

"There's just one thing I want to ask you," Annalise said when they were back outside the café.

"What's that?" Chas asked. He seemed fine again, once more the congenial, even charming man she thought she'd been getting to know. Until she'd smelled that wind blowing.

"Are you crazy?"

He turned and gave her a long, steady look. The corners of his mouth quirked. "I used to be." Heading for the car, he added, "But I'm much better now."

Chapter 9

"Where's the nearest hardware store?" Chas asked as he pulled away from the curb.

Preoccupied with the thought that she just might have made the mistake of her life by involving him, Annalise didn't respond at once. She was too busy thinking about this man who had saved her from the goons, sent her senses reeling and faced down Brad Fuller. Was he the tough but essentially gentle man she'd thought she'd glimpsed, or the lightning-wind stranger with the keen edge of violence shimmering around him?

And while she was on the subject, what did "much better now" mean?

"Annalise?"

She jumped slightly, realizing he'd said something. "What?"

He repeated himself patiently. More than that, he even looked a little amused.

"That big building down at the end of the street," she replied. "What are we going there for?"

"Stuff," he said

Half an hour later, Annalise looked at the stack of supplies he'd picked out. She had the grace to be just a little embarrassed by the car batteries. He'd found them right away, but had taken half a dozen instead of just the one he needed. And he'd added a whole lot of other things, from gallon-size bottles of detergent to sacks of fertilizer, coils of insulated wire, tar paper, roof shingles, a carton of firecrackers left over from the previous Fourth of July and even several dozen glass jars with screw-on lids for putting up preserves.

"I don't get it," she said. "What do we need with all this?"

"Long as I'm here, I thought I'd do a little work around the place."

"You don't have to—"

"I like to keep busy."

And that, it seemed, settled that. As she helped him haul their purchases out to the car, she made up her mind. "Okay, that's it. I know I made a deal, but I have to know what you're planning."

Chas laughed, a deep, slightly rough sound that sent a shiver of pleasure down her spine. "I wondered how long you were going to hold out. Let's make a couple more stops, then head back to the ranch and I'll fill you in."

Grudgingly, Annalise agreed. After a whirlwind fifteen minutes buying groceries, they pulled into the parking lot in front of the Pecos Bar and Grill. Chas got out, took one of the batteries and headed for his car. As he propped the hood up and started to work, Annalise sat, fidgeting until she couldn't stand it anymore.

"Here," she said, coming up beside him, "let me do that." Quickly and efficiently, she disconnected the damaged battery and hooked up its replacement.

"Looks like you could do that with your eyes closed," Chas said when she was done.

"I think I have," Annalise admitted. "I worked as a mechanic through most of college."

"You did?" He couldn't hide his surprise.

"I love cars, always have since I was a kid, and it paid a whole lot better than other jobs." She'd met guys who were really threatened when they found out that she'd succeeded at an occupation they liked to think of as their own. But Chas wasn't among them. He merely nodded.

"Makes sense," he said, and slammed the hood back down. "I'll follow you back."

They reached the ranch without incident. Annalise went to check on the horses grazing in the paddocks. When she got back, Chas had finished unloading the supplies into a spare corner of the barn. He was just setting the last battery down when she came in.

Dust motes danced in the light filtering through cracks in the walls. The air smelled sweetly of hay and leather. It was very quiet.

He was wearing a cotton shirt that stretched tautly over the muscles of his back as he bent. So, too, did his khakis stretch, providing Annalise with a new and interesting insight into the fondness some women expressed for the masculine posterior. For the first time that she could remember, she felt the same way.

He straightened, rubbing the back of his neck.

"Tired?" she asked.

"Not really, just thinking."

His hair looked like dark gold, a strand falling over his forehead, and his eyes were shadowed. She couldn't really make them out. But she could see his mouth clearly. It was firm and inviting, with that little quirk at the corners that appeared when he was amused.

She glanced away hastily. "How about some lunch?"

"I'll cook."

Annalise laughed. "You make it sound like I threatened you."

"Let's just say I worry more about letting you loose in a kitchen than I do about our friend Fuller."

"You're going to tell me why, aren't you?" she urged as they walked back toward the house.

"Look," Chas began when they were settled in the kitchen, "we already know the guy's dangerous. Nobody blows up a truck because they're having a bad hair day, much less sends his boys to commit felony kidnapping. So the question is, is he also stupid? My current bet is no."

"Weren't you the one who said I could be betting with my life?"

"To which you replied that you weren't going to turn tail and run."

"Fair enough. Okay, dangerous but not stupid. So what?"

"He wants something that involves getting you off this land or at least getting you to sell it to him. What could that be?"

Annalise shook her head. It was a little distracting trying to think while his strong, sinewed hands were making short work of a head of lettuce and chopping up a carrot with heart-stopping speed. But she managed. "I've got no idea. To be honest, I haven't really thought about it."

"Start. How much land does Fuller already own?"

"About four thousand acres, all together."

"How big is this place?"

"Five hundred acres, counting what I rent out."

"Hardly seems worth his while."

"No, it doesn't," she agreed. "All I've been able to focus on is that he wants my land. But now that you bring it up, I can't see why he would."

"Maybe he's just land crazy."

"Maybe, except there are plenty of places for sale around here. People have taken a real beating in recent years. If he's willing to pay fifty thousand dollars, he'd have would-be sellers knocking down his door."

"So it's just this place he wants," Chas said. "Tell me about it."

"There's nothing to tell. I think it's the most beautiful spot on earth, but my opinion's probably a minority of one."

"Why are you so attached to it?"

She hesitated, not sure how to put it into words. "I was a lonely kid. Both my folks worked the horse shows, and weeks would go by when I wouldn't see them. I stayed here with Uncle Tris. He was father, mother, teacher, friend—everything."

"You were lucky to have him," Chas said quietly. A shadow, bleak in its intensity, moved behind his eyes. It was gone quickly, but not before Annalise wondered what could possibly have caused it.

"Loving your uncle isn't the same as loving this land."

"No, but he taught me to really appreciate it. There's a . . . a rhythm to this place, a way of coexisting with nature that you have to experience to really understand."

"While he was coexisting, did your uncle do anything else? Mining, for instance?"

"Mining? For what?"

"Gold, minerals, gems, anything?"

She shook her head emphatically. "No, there was nothing like that. He raised horses, same as me."

"Could there have been something else and you just didn't know about it?"

"Believe me, if Uncle Tris had been mining for gold—or anything else—he wouldn't have been able to keep it to himself."

"Then there has to be another explanation. I don't think Fuller's a crackpot. He's got a reason for wanting this land." Chas dumped the lettuce in a bowl, added the carrot and turned his attention to making sandwiches. Annalise watched in unwilling fascination as he spread mayonnaise and horseradish on pumpernickel, added sliced tomatoes and onion and finished off with roast beef.

"Let's eat," he said as he carried the plates to the table. She followed with the salad and drinks. Moments later, her eyes were squeezed shut in unfeigned pleasure as the first bite of the sandwich made its way across her tongue.

"This is the best sandwich I've ever had," she said, and meant it.

"I'd take that as a compliment but I've got some idea of what you're used to eating. How was Uncle Tris at cooking?"

"Depends," she said. "He made chili that could peel the paint off walls." Proudly she added, "And he taught me how to make it, too."

"I live for the experience. So you grew up eating death chili, raising horses and roaming over this land. After lunch, suppose you show it to me."

"The chili?"

He raised his eyebrows in mock dismay. "It's still around? No, I meant the land."

"It's hard riding. Cars won't make it."

"That's all right," he said quietly, and went back to his sandwich, leaving her to contemplate the wisdom of wandering across the place she loved best with a man who, moment by moment, shattered the sense of peace she had always found there.

Chapter 10

He rode well, sitting easily in the saddle with a light hold on the reins. Falcon, the stallion Annalise had picked for Chas, seemed to like him. He perked up his ears and danced along, to the amusement of the man astride him.

"Good horse," he said, patting Falcon's neck with easy affection. "You train him?"

From atop her favorite mare, Wind Dancer, Annalise nodded. She didn't completely buy the notion that you could tell a great deal about a man from the way he treated animals, but the firm gentleness with which Chas handled the big horse impressed her nonetheless.

They rode out along a narrow trail that cut between the hills to the west of the ranch and the stream that ran near them. The day was perfect, washed clean by the previous night's rain and cooler than the weather had been lately.

When Annalise commented on that, Chas said, "How have you been doing for rain around here?"

"Not too bad, but water can still be a problem, the same as it is all through these parts."

"Where do you get most of yours from?"

"Wells."

"They ever run dry?"

"A few years ago when the drought was going on, one of them did."

"Has Fuller had more, or less, water than you?"

"About the same or maybe less. If you're thinking he wants this land for the water under it, I just don't see that."

"It was a long shot," Chas admitted. The trail narrowed. He rode ahead; Annalise followed. They continued for about a quarter mile before the trail widened again and they could ride side by side. A short distance beyond, they came out at the head of a canyon.

The hills rose above them, streaked apricot and blue-gray, black and gold in the slanting sun. Birds flitted about their high perches. In the tumbled bushes that hugged the stream, small animals scurried.

"This is a beautiful place," Chas said softly.

"It's my favorite. There's just something about it. I always feel better coming here."

"I can see why."

They started deeper into the canyon. The shadows grew longer as the silence wrapped around them. The only sound was the soft clop of the horses' hooves and the whisper of wind between the canyon walls.

A small stream rose within the canyon. Where its waters bubbled out of the ground, they paused to let the horses drink. Annalise swung a leg over Wind Dancer's rump and started to dismount. Strong hands closed around her waist. She stiffened but did not object. Chas lowered her to the ground and stood, still holding her, for a long moment.

She was tall for a woman, but he was taller still. She had to tip her head to look at him. They were very close, so much so that she could see the pulse that leapt in his jaw.

"Annalise..." Her name was a rough caress. His hand splayed out at the small of her back. The other rested lightly on the curve of her hip.

He smelled of crisp cotton, leather and horse, and the wild scent of the canyon itself whispering through timeless caverns. The broad span of his chest and shoulders blotted out the sun. She was suddenly disoriented, confused, overwhelmed by emotions that had always before been kept in strictest check.

Without thought, hardly realizing what she was doing, she braced her hands against his chest. He was all warm, rock-hard muscle and sinew, vibrant with life, compelling in his masculinity. Her breath caught. She moved, heedlessly, against him.

He made a sound deep in his throat and tightened his hold. Hips brushing his, she was suddenly, unmistakably aware that she was not alone in the desire coursing through her. He shared it fully. For just a moment, alarm almost overcame passion. But the strength she felt in him, and the stability, soothed her fears.

She might regret it later, but in this instant of time, free of all the usual restrictions, she desperately needed to stand in the shadows of the canyon, in the arms of this man, in the hot, sweet languor of the moment.

His head bent. She felt the brush of his lips, hard yet gentle. Her own parted in response. In that moment, all things were possible, even inevitable.

Abruptly it changed. After that first, tentative touch, they both hesitated. Chas dropped his hands; Annalise did the same. They both took a quick step apart.

"I'm sorry," he said. "I didn't mean for that—"

"Me, either," she assured him. What in heaven's name had gotten into her? She'd never been particularly forward with men and certainly not with one she hardly knew.

"I wouldn't want you to think—" he said.

"Oh, I don't. Not at all. Let's just forget it."

He nodded, but his eyes were shadowed and the silence that descended between them was strained.

Glad of the distraction Wind Dancer offered, Annalise busied herself by leading the mare to drink and loosening her saddle girths. Chas did the same for Falcon. When both horses were grazing, he joined her beside the stream.

Softly, so as not to disturb the fragile peace, Chas asked, "Is this where the Anasazi ruins are?"

Annalise shook her head. It was absurd to feel so uncomfortable. These things happened. They'd both realized it was ill-advised and they'd both drawn back.

If Chas was going to be staying for a while—and she allowed herself no second thoughts about that—they had to get back on a more normal footing.

"They're about a mile east of here," she said matter-of-factly, "on land Fuller owned before he donated it to the National Park Service."

"Sounds out of character."

"He got a tax write-off."

"That explains it. Do you climb?"

"About as far as the third step on the ladder. Why?"

He shaded his eyes and glanced up along the canyon walls. "I was thinking this would be a good place to do some rock climbing."

Annalise followed the direction of his gaze. She had a sudden, fragmented image of herself clinging to the sheer rock. A wave of coldness washed over her. "I realize people have all sorts of ideas about what's fun, but I'll pass."

He nodded, but continued to study the rock face. There, in the canyon, he looked perfectly content. The coiled violence she'd felt earlier seemed never to have been. In its place was a faint, lingering sadness.

"What's wrong?" she asked quietly.

He turned, surprised. "Wrong?"

She shrugged, downplaying her perceptiveness. It didn't seem appropriate—or even possible—to be so attuned to a man she'd known such a short time. "You looked a little sad, that's all."

He was silent for a moment, deciding what to say. "I was thinking about my son, Jimmy. He'd love to see this."

"Your son? I didn't realize . . ."

"His mother and I are divorced."

He'd had a life entirely apart from all that wandering he'd done, a life involving a woman and a child. She should have realized that, should have guessed that a man of his innate virility and strength wouldn't have lived like a monk.

They were silent as they remounted. Long moments passed before Annalise spoke again.

"How old is Jimmy?" she asked softly.

"Six." The sudden, sweeping tenderness in his eyes made her breath catch. "He lives in Michigan with my ex-wife and her husband."

"Do you see him?" She'd heard so many horrible stories about children separated from parents, sometimes for good reason, but often just because the grown-ups couldn't find a way to get along decently enough.

"I do now. We were on a camping trip together right before I came down here." His smile was filled with quiet pride. "He really loves the outdoors. Says he wants to be an ecologist."

"You really love him, don't you?" It was too personal a remark, especially under the circumstances, but it was also a truth so self-evident that it couldn't be denied.

He glanced away, but for just an instant she thought she caught the sheen of moisture in his eyes. "Yes, I really do."

"It's a shame . . . I mean, it's none of my business, but it's too bad you can't be with him all the time."

Chas straightened in the saddle, the momentary vulnerability gone as quickly as it had come. "Lisa married a great guy. His name's Mark. Jimmy couldn't have a better father."

"Don't you mean stepfather?"

His face tightened. "I wasn't a father to Jimmy when he was younger. Mark was the first real father he'd ever known. I'm grateful to be in my son's life now, but I don't have any illusions. Mark will always be his father in the ways that count the most."

She thought of how her uncle had been there for her, how lovingly he had filled the void left by parents who weren't around. "I'm glad for Jimmy."

"So am I," Chas said and clearly meant it. There was no resentment or rancor in him, only acceptance that what was best for the child had to come ahead of everything else. It was a side of his personality she hadn't glimpsed before and it went a long way toward strengthening her confidence in him.

There was just one little point...

She cleared her throat. "By the way, back in town, what was that you meant?"

"About what?"

"Being 'much better now.' Was that a joke?"

He gave her a long, level look. Perhaps it was the lingering effect of his thoughts about Jimmy, but there was a sort of wry affection in his eyes as they swept over her. The corners of his mouth lifted. "Sure it was. Come on, let's ride a little farther."

She went, following him along the narrow canyon floor where bluebonnets clustered and the scent of wild grasses drifted on the air. Eventually, the opening widened, the cliffs fell away and they emerged onto the plateau. The sun was fading westward. Only a few hours of daylight remained.

"We'd better get back," Chas said. "I've got a few things to do before dark." Turning, they headed for the ranch.

Chapter 11

"What's that?" Annalise asked. She was standing a couple of yards inside the split-rail fence that ran in front of the house. Chas was crouched down with a spool of wire in one hand and a staple gun in the other. The yard all the way around the house was dotted with short sticks set a few feet apart and protruding several inches above the ground. Chas was methodically stringing the wire between them.

It was getting on for dusk. Except for the five minutes he'd taken to put on a pot of potatoes, he'd been busy with the supplies they'd bought.

For a while, she'd watched him from the front window of the room she used as an office. There was always paperwork to be done for any business, but she usually managed to plow through it more efficiently than she was doing now. She'd fill in a line or two, punch up a couple of numbers on her computer and find herself watching Chas again. Finally, when she couldn't stand it any longer, she gave up and went outside.

"This?" he said. "Just a little surprise for anybody who happens to come by without an invitation."

Annalise frowned. She couldn't really see how wire and sticks were going to have much impact. But just as she was about to ask, her nose twitched. The potatoes. Turning, she ran for the house, leaving Chas laughing behind her.

She got the potatoes out of the pan and dumped them in a colander, ran cold water over them and left them to sit. That done, she was heading back out to the yard when the phone rang.

She picked up on the second ring, crooking the receiver against her shoulder while keeping an eye out the window. Chas was still working. He'd taken off his shirt. Smooth muscles worked under burnished skin. The man was a menace.

"Yes?" she murmured, hardly aware of what she said.

"Sorry to disturb you." The voice was low and husky with the loose gravel sound of cigars and corn whiskey, late nights and dreams gone awry. It wasn't an unpleasant voice, just a tired one, world-weary, the voice of a man set on going through the motions, getting through one more day.

Annalise closed her eyes for a moment, summoning patience. She had a strong sense that she was about to get angry and had to remind herself that it wouldn't do any good.

"How are you, Sheriff?" she asked casually, as she would have several months ago before the trouble had started. As though he hadn't turned her away when her truck had blown up, making it clear that her problems were strictly her own.

"I hear you've got company," Billy Joe Jethro said. He was out of Arkansas originally, having had a long stint in the U.S. Navy and a couple of years on a big-city police force. That hadn't agreed with him— something about a drug bust gone sour. He'd decided he liked small-town living better. Most people around Pecos liked him right back. He didn't give speeding tickets, let drunks sleep it off in the town jail without busting them and generally minded his own business.

Not now, though. Now, all of a sudden, he was minding Annalise's.

"Funny about that," she said. "I got the impression you didn't much care about anything that went on around here."

Billy Joe cleared his throat. She thought she heard him take a drink of something and wondered what it was. He wasn't known for drinking on the job, just in between, but today might be an exception. He was shaping his words very carefully, as though each one had to fit together with the others exactly so, or they might all fall apart.

"I'm just trying to be a friend," he said.

She shook her head, disgusted. The anger was bubbling up, resisting her best efforts. "Come off it. Fuller got you to do this. Is he sitting right there with

you, Billy Joe, yanking on your leash? Or is he so sure
of you that he's actually letting you do this by yourself?''

There was a long silence, then he sighed deeply, like
a man whose one remaining conviction is that nobody can be saved. ''There's no call for that, Annalise. It's not gonna do you any good. Truth is I don't
much care what you think of me. I'm just trying to
stop you from making a really bad mistake.''

''I already made one when I thought you'd stand up
for the law around here. You wouldn't and I don't
much like being hung out to dry, so I got some help.''

''Yeah, well he'd better be Rambo and the Termi-
nator rolled into one, sweetheart, 'cause Fuller's spit-
tin' mad. He's liable to go and do something foolish.''

A cold dart of fear ran down Annalise's spine,
curled around the bottom of her feet and shot back up
again. She tightened her grip on the phone. ''You tell
him that would be *his* really bad mistake.''

''Sure, I'll tell him. He'll listen to me about as well
as you do. Just don't say nobody warned you.''

''You're a prince, Billy Joe, a real credit to the
drinking profession. Let me ask you something, if it's
not too much trouble. Could you get your mind off
how many minutes it's going to be before you get hold
of a bottle and give some thought to why Fuller's doing this?''

Silence again and the static of the phone line like
wind whistling across a distant prairie. Slowly Billy
Joe said, ''He wants your land.''

"I *know* that. For God's sake, there can't be a six-year-old within a hundred miles of here who doesn't know that by now. *Why* does he want it?"

"I . . . have no idea." There was a faint note of curiosity in his voice, as if he'd just realized there ought to be a reason for a man to go around harassing a woman, blowing up her truck, trying to get her kidnapped and now planning who-knew-what kind of mayhem.

But the notion apparently faded as quickly as it arose. "Who cares?" he asked, the equivalent of a verbal shrug. "Fuller's gonna do whatever he wants. He doesn't need a reason."

"That's nuts."

"Yeah, maybe, so what?"

"It doesn't bother you any, a crazy man running around messing everything up and threatening people?"

"No," Billy Joe said slowly. He seemed sure about this at least. "That's just how things are."

"Maybe in your world, but not in mine. If Fuller comes at me again, he's going to regret it. Make sure you tell him that, Billy Joe. Whether he hears you or not, you tell him. And you tell his men, too, because if it comes down to it, they're the ones you're going to be scraping off the ground."

Brave words when brave was the last thing she was feeling. That hard, cold tingling had settled in the pit of her stomach. Any minute now, she was going to lose it.

"I've got to go," she said. "If you have any more friendly advice, keep it to yourself."

She hung up and wiped her damp palm on the leg of her jeans. Her heart was thudding and her breathing sounded labored, as though she'd run miles. It was very quiet in the kitchen, but just beyond, she could hear the soft call of a bird bidding farewell to day.

Outside the windows, across the yard, the sun was going down in glory. She walked out into it, head high, not running, walking steadily and purposefully to Chas. All she could think of right at that moment was how glad she was that he was there. And how guilty she felt that she'd involved him.

"How's it going?" she asked as he straightened up, the spool empty in his hand.

His eyes narrowed slightly, scanning her. "Okay."

"That's good. We may have some real trouble."

"You didn't burn those potatoes, did you?"

Startled, she looked up at him through the gathering shadows and saw that he was teasing her. Absurdly, her eyes filled with tears. "The potatoes are fine. That was the sheriff on the phone. I gather we can expect a visit from Fuller."

Chas shook his head. He took her arm so lightly that she hardly knew it and began walking toward the barn. "He won't come."

"Yeah, I think he will."

"He's a coward. He'll send somebody else, just like he did yesterday."

"Him, his men—what difference does it make?"

"Man never fights as hard for something that isn't really his."

In the shadow of the barn, in the gathering dusk, he stopped, hesitating. Even to her untutored gaze, he seemed a man caught between contradictory impulses. Gently his fingers curled under her chin. Time seemed to slow down, to pause. She could have drawn back, could have turned away, but she did neither. There was a sense of rightness to all this, as though they had been heading toward it all along. Instead, her head lifted, her eyes meeting his. In the hay-scented air, something ancient and primal moved between them.

He made a sound deep in his throat and wrapped a steely arm around her waist. Her hands flattened out on his chest, not pushing him away but tracing with her palms and fingertips the contours of hard muscle and sinew. She could feel the heat of his skin, the moisture smooth against it where he had labored hard, protecting her.

The coldness in her stomach melted but fear lingered, not of Fuller and certainly not of Billy Joe. It was fear that this moment, this man, this sudden, unexpected vision of what life could be like, would be taken from her with as little warning as it had all been given.

Desire for the land warred with yearning for the man. It was impossible to say which would have won if his mouth hadn't come down and silenced anything she might have said.

Chapter 12

It was stupid to touch her, bone-deep stupid, the kind of flat-out dumbness that could get a man killed. Or a woman. He knew that less than a second after the sweet warmth of her mouth melted under his but he still couldn't seem to do much about it.

She was so tempting, so alive and giving, so real in a way he couldn't remember feeling in—how long? Maybe never. He'd been alone a long time and before that, after the breakup with Lisa, had had only brief, joyless relationships that left him more unsatisfied than anything else.

This was different. He had no words for it, nothing but the gut-wrenching knowledge that he was suddenly vulnerable in a way he could not have imagined. Nothing he knew or had experienced could have prepared him for what he was feeling.

Slowly he raised his head. Her eyes were dark and slumberous, her mouth slightly swollen. He could feel the rapid-fire beat of her heart against his own and knew that he was no steadier than she. The barn was dark and quiet. It would have been so very easy to lower her into the hay, strip off their clothes and surrender to the passion they both so clearly felt.

So easy. He drew a deep, ragged breath and held it for a moment before letting it out slowly. In a voice he barely recognized as his own, he said, "We'd better get back to work."

He saw her wince, as though the sudden return to reality was as unsettling to her as it was to him. A shutter fell over her expression, hiding her thoughts. She took a quick step backward.

"Yes, we'd better."

Neither moved. They looked past each other at the rough-hewn walls of the barn with the last rays of sunlight filtering through them. The muscles of her slender throat worked as she swallowed.

He turned away quickly, before he could think about what it would feel like to press his lips to her skin just there where the vein throbbed, to slowly trace his mouth down to—

"Over here," he said and pointed to the table of sawhorses and wood planks that he'd set up at the far end of the barn.

"What's this?" she asked, staring at what he'd laid out there.

"The detergent and fertilizer need to be mixed together. I'll give you the proportions. We can use the funnel I bought and those clean containers. Each of the glass jars has to be filled two-thirds of the way.

After that, we'll poke a hole in the lid of each jar and thread a piece of cloth into it.''

Annalise's eyes widened. She looked at him in frank disbelief. ''What're we talking about here—Molotov cocktails?''

''Those are made from gasoline and they're a hell of a lot more dangerous. These produce a terrific bang and some flame, but they're much less likely to cause serious injury.''

''I still don't like the idea that anyone can go into their friendly neighborhood store and buy the ingredients for what amounts to a bomb.''

''If you want a bomb, there's a third item you have to add that we're not going to talk about. Besides, the fertilizer has to be processed before it's useful. I'll do that part.''

''I see,'' she said slowly. ''Actually, I don't. Did you pick up this particular skill when you were working in the sugar refinery or on the fishing trawler? Or maybe it was during the stint in Brazil training horses?''

''Argentina. Look, I've bummed around a lot and I've learned one or two things that occasionally come in useful. Now either you want to be a sitting duck or you don't. Which is it?''

The play of emotion across her face was expressive. Clearly, she was torn between a horror of violence and the understandable desire not to be a victim of it. If he could have spared her such a decision, he would gladly have done so. But he hadn't written the rules—Fuller had. All Chas could do was play to win.

''Let's get this done,'' she said and turned back to the table.

* * *

An hour later, Chas called a halt. The glass jars were filled and set out on the porch. The horses had been removed from the stables and left to graze overnight in the paddock at the farthest distance from the house. They weren't used to that, but they'd do all right.

He checked the wire one last time, brushed his hands off and went in the side door to the kitchen. Annalise was sitting at the table. She was cleaning a rifle.

Chas frowned. "What's that for?"

She didn't look up, just kept on working. Her movements were a little clumsy, as though she didn't do this sort of thing all that often. "What do you think?"

"Put it away."

That got her attention. She lowered the gun, looked up and met his gaze squarely. "Unless you were lying about what you've got in the trunk of your car, this is the only real weapon around here."

"It's a peashooter. Put it away."

Her face was very pale. She had bitten her bottom lip so that a tiny rim of blood shone against it. "If Fuller's boys are really coming, they're going to be armed."

"And at the first sight, or sound, of a gun, they'll feel justified letting loose with everything they've got. Is that what you want?"

"No, but..."

"There are no buts. You agreed that we handle this my way."

She hesitated, but her hand was still on the gun. "In case you haven't noticed, I'm not exactly the compliant type."

"Think of it as a learning experience."

"Oh, it's that, all right."

Gently he reached over and took the rifle from her. A quick check was enough to confirm that it was unloaded.

She saw what he was doing and grimaced. "I'm not stupid, either."

"Anybody can make a mistake."

"Cleaning a loaded rifle is right up there with—"

"Falling asleep at the wheel of a car."

"What?"

"It's hard to believe it was only yesterday that I started to doze off behind the wheel and decided I needed to stop somewhere."

"Somewhere being the Pecos Bar and Grill?"

"The one, the only."

A soft laugh escaped her. "You sure can pick 'em."

"I didn't used to think so," he said, looking straight at her. "But now I'm more inclined to agree." He propped the gun up against the wall and put his hands on her shoulders, deliberately keeping his touch reassuring but nonsexual. It wasn't easy. In fact, it was impossible. But he did try.

"Speaking of learning experiences . . ."

A slight flush crept over her cheeks. "What?"

"I'm going to teach you to make potato salad," he said, and before she could respond, he set her briskly on her feet and tossed her a towel. "Put this around your waist. It can get messy."

"I'll bet," she muttered, but followed him over to the counter. As she set to work peeling the potatoes, she said, "Just think, killer chili, potato salad and Molotov cocktails. Sorry, non-Molotov. Talk about a party no one would ever forget."

"Try leaving some of the potato. Steaks okay?"

"I could choke one down. Did your ex-wife cook?"

The question caught him unawares. He'd been surprised to find himself telling her about Jimmy, much less Lisa and Mark. They were something he didn't usually discuss with anyone.

Maybe it was the fond memory of the days he'd just spent with Jimmy, or maybe it was that Annalise was so easy to talk with. Whatever the reason, he shrugged lightly and said, "Yeah, she did. Where's the pepper?"

"Over there."

He thought she was going to ask something more, had himself braced for it, but she seemed focused on the potatoes, diligently trying to get the skins off without taking everything else with them. Her brow was wrinkled slightly. He suppressed an urge to smooth it out and set to work on the steaks.

Chapter 13

"I'll take the first watch," Chas said.

Dinner was over. They had finished cleaning up, and the house was very quiet. There was no hint, not the merest inkling that anything could possibly be wrong.

Until he spoke, and the words, like a rush of cold water, reminded Annalise of the danger she had managed to block out for a short time at least.

Of course, there would have to be watches. They couldn't possibly both go to sleep and risk being caught off guard. Full of steak and conversation, paradoxically more relaxed than she had been in a very long time, she was abashedly glad he'd offered to go first. It was all she could do to keep her eyes open.

And yet, after she'd said goodnight and made her way upstairs, fatigue fell away and she was left almost painfully alert. She took a quick shower, toweled her hair dry and tried to decide what to do.

She was due to relieve Chas at 3:00 a.m. and knew she had to be alert. But the thought of trying to sleep held no appeal. As a compromise, she dressed again in comfortable jeans and a shirt, set her boots on the floor beside the bed and lay down on top of the covers. To be on the safe side, she set the alarm clock, but she didn't seriously expect to need it.

For an hour or so she tossed and turned, drifting between a light state that hardly even qualified as sleep and full wakefulness. But at length, the long day and the larger-than-usual meal took their toll, and she slipped into deep slumber.

"Annalise."

The voice was soft but firm, calling to her through dreams. She turned over reluctantly and tried to swat it away.

"Annalise." More strongly now, insisting. Reluctantly she was drawn upward. Her eyes flickered, once, twice, and opened.

Chas was there beside the bed, a solid, formidable presence garbed in shadow. She raised herself, balanced on her elbows and tried to remember why he was there, what was happening.

"You need to get up."

Memory surfaced. Startled, she looked at the clock, thinking she had overslept. But the luminescent dial read 2:00 a.m. She wasn't due to relieve him for another hour.

With that came the realization of why he had to be standing there, why he had awakened her.

She sat up with a jolt and swung her legs over the side of the bed. Chas laid a cautionary hand on her shoulder. "Very quietly. They're outside, but they haven't made a move yet."

Silently she nodded. Her heart was in her throat, but she managed to get her boots on and followed him out of the room. All the lights were off. Together they made their way downstairs and to the windows at the front of the house.

"I heard a pickup about five minutes ago," Chas whispered. "They left it over there in the trees." He pointed to a spot about a hundred yards from the house.

"How many of them are there?" Strange to hear herself ask so sensible a question when terror threatened, licking the edges of her soul. It was one thing to know this might happen, even to anticipate it. But to wake in darkness to the reality of danger, that was entirely different.

"Six, I think," Chas said. "Not more."

"You were right, then."

"How's that?"

"You said he'd send more men next time."

He squeezed her arm reassuringly. "We're ready for them. Here, take this." He handed her a lighter, the kind you could pick up anywhere for a couple of dollars. There'd been a display of them beside the cash register at the hardware store. Belatedly, she remembered that he'd tossed a couple into their cart.

"When you light one of the jars," he said, "Hold it just long enough to count to ten like this—one and two and three and so on. Not rushed, but not dragging it out either. Then rear your arm back and give that sucker a long, hard throw. Don't worry about what you're aiming for, it won't matter. Just try to loft it out over the fence."

"All right," she said doubtfully. She couldn't imagine herself using such a weapon, but she had the feeling that was about to change.

"Here they come," Chas said. He crouched down behind the window, pulling her with him.

Everything happened very fast after that. She could feel her own breathing, the rapid thud of her heart, the warmth and strength of Chas against her. Then a muttered curse split the night, an exclamation of surprise followed suddenly by an explosion of sound. Instinctively, she flinched and covered her head with her arms. Loud pops were going off one after another, men were shouting, there were screams.

Chas leapt up. "Come on," he said and pulled her to her feet. Together, they raced out onto the porch. He grabbed one of the jars, lit the cloth fuse, counted, then lofted it in a clean line out into the darkness.

Annalise's hands were shaking, but she did the same. Explosions like small-arms fire were still going off throughout the yard. Fuller's men were running around in confusion. She saw two or three with their guns out, but they had no idea what was happening or where to fire.

Just then the first jar exploded. Fire lit the night sky. Annalise took a deep breath, sought the cool center of calm deep within her and flicked the lighter.

It was over quickly. They lit barely half a dozen of the containers they had prepared. Before the last one's flames had died away, Fuller's men were on the run. None appeared to be injured, but they were all clearly in the grip of stark terror.

"It's a damned army!" one shouted as he dove headfirst over the fence, lurched to his feet and raced out of sight.

Standing on the porch, Annalise slowly lowered the unlit jar she was holding. With great care, she set it off to the side. Slowly she straightened.

Chas grinned at her. He looked suddenly very young, his hair windblown and a streak of dirt down his face. He put an arm around her shoulders, drew her to him and kissed her hard on the mouth.

"What do you know," he said when he'd raised his head. "It worked."

Dazed, not quite sure if she was still standing, Annalise murmured, "Try not to sound so surprised."

There was a pop when the wire setting off the last of the fireworks was tripped. Annalise jumped. Chas put an arm around her waist. Together they went back into the house.

Chapter 14

"I figure we've gained at least a few days," Chas said. It was shortly after dawn. They had cleaned up the yard, disposing of the wire and remnants of the firecrackers, and had hidden the remaining jars under the hay in the barn. The horses were back in the paddock beside the stables. There was orange juice and toast on the table. Everything looked remarkably normal. Nothing remained to show what had happened during the night except for the strain on their faces.

"You think so?" Annalise asked. She had scrambled eggs. Remarkably, they weren't burnt. Ladling them onto the plates, she added, "Fuller's going to be madder than ever."

"Yeah, but his men aren't going to be in any hurry

to do what he wants now. You heard what one of them said."

She nodded. "He thought we were an army." A smile flickered across her face. "I guess that's really how it seemed to them."

"Confusion is a great weapon. There's no telling whether those guys actually headed back to Fuller's place or if they just kept on going. Either way, he's going to have a hell of a time convincing anybody to try this again."

"Then we've won."

"Not exactly. I don't see Fuller throwing up his hands and forgetting the whole thing. Do you?"

"No," she admitted as she sat down across from him.

She was so tired, her vision was starting to blur, but at the same time she felt more alive than she ever had before. "What do you suppose he'll do next?" she asked glumly.

"Beats me. Our best bet is to figure out why he's doing any of this at all. Until we do that, we're going to have to keep on worrying about him."

He said "we" so easily, she thought, as though they really were both facing this. She had to keep reminding herself that he was hired help. This was no time to get comfortable. Sooner or later, Chas would be moving on and she'd be left alone to face whatever remained. The thought was enough to quash whatever relief she'd been feeling.

"Maybe he's just plain crazy," she suggested, moving her eggs around on the plate. Her appetite seemed to have deserted her.

"I don't think so."

"Are you sure?"

He smiled faintly. "Does this come under the heading of 'It takes one to know one'?"

She flushed. "I didn't mean anything like that. I just can't think of a single reason why he would be so determined to get hold of my land."

"Did your uncle leave any records?"

She thought for a moment. "Only the usual stuff. Stud books, feed bills—things like that."

"Nothing else?"

"Not that I know of."

"I suggest we start looking, but first we both need some rest."

Annalise agreed. They cleaned up the breakfast dishes and stood around a little awkwardly, neither willing to leave the other but reluctant to press the issue, either, when the sound of a car engine coming up the road gave them a reprieve.

Chas went to the door and looked out. "Offhand, I'd guess this is Billy Joe Jethro."

Annalise peered around his shoulder. "Yep, that's him."

"Doesn't look too good."

In fact, the sheriff looked as though he'd been on a ten-day drunk. His uniform was wrinkled, his hair needed a wash, his jaw was unshaven and he shambled slightly as he walked. Inside the gate, he paused and took a long look around. He was still doing that when Chas opened the door and stepped out.

"Something I can do for you?" he asked.

Jethro peered at him. He scratched his head. "Funny, you don't look like they said."

"How's that?"

"Ten feet tall and spitting fire."

Chas shrugged modestly. "A man can get a little mixed-up when too much is happening all at once."

"I suppose," Jethro said doubtfully. He looked at Annalise. "How're you doing?"

"Just fine, thanks."

"Have any trouble?"

Annalise and Chas exchanged a quick look. Slowly she shook her head. "No, can't say as we did."

Jethro frowned. He rubbed his hand over his face as though trying to clear it. "That's not what Fuller's men say."

"Oh, yeah?" Chas asked. He looked mildly interested.

"Yeah, they claim there was a big fight out here last night, you and maybe a dozen other guys against them. They claim you were armed to the teeth, semi-automatics at the least plus some kind of grenades. Funny, though," he went on, glancing around. "Place sure doesn't look like it got shot up."

"Sounds like the boys have been hitting the moonshine a little hard," Annalise suggested.

Billy Joe winced. The idea struck a little too close to home. "They dragged me out of bed in the middle of the night acting like an army was on their tails. How am I supposed to believe nothing happened?"

"Middle of the night?" Chas repeated. He grinned at Annalise. "Took you a while to come by."

"Figured I'd give it time to settle down, whatever it was." He looked at them both more closely. "You *sure* nothing happened?"

"Nothing worth mentioning," Chas said. "If those boys think something did, they better think again. Believe me, when something really does go down, they won't be hanging around to talk about it."

"I'll be sure and tell them that," Jethro muttered. He shot them a final glance and headed back to his car.

Behind him, Annalise sagged with relief. "He bought it." She hesitated. "Didn't he?"

"Depends. Does he think something scared the be-jeesus out of Fuller's men? Sure he does. Does he know what it was? Not on your life."

"How long do you suppose he'll go on wondering?"

"Forever, if he can. Billy Joe Jethro doesn't strike me as the sort who goes looking for trouble. He'll be happy to stay out of here."

"And Fuller's men?"

"He's going to have to do some recruiting and that will take time."

She sighed deeply. "I guess we'd better make the most of it."

He was standing very close, not touching her, but that didn't seem to matter. She could feel him along every inch of her being.

"The bunkhouse is probably dry by now," he said.

"There's always the guest room," she countered.

Still, neither moved. Long moments passed during which the only motion was that of the rays of sunlight sliding gently through the windows. Finally, Chas gave a deep sigh. He bent with easy grace, lifted her into his arms and mounted the stairs.

Chapter 15

Annalise murmured softly and turned over in her sleep. She was warm, content and deliciously relaxed. A smile curved her mouth. Eyes still closed, she reached out instinctively and touched—not smooth covers and the familiar contours of her bed, but something solid, rock-hard, real. Some*one*.

Her eyes opened. She sat up quickly and stared at the man beside her. Chas lay on his side, facing her. He was bare chested, the covers pushed down to his waist. His hair was tousled and his thick lashes cast shadows over his cheeks. Asleep, he looked younger, less the formidable, even dangerous, man she was coming to know and more the boy she imagined he might have been.

But imagination was a dangerous thing. With very little effort, she could imagine what it would feel like to brush aside the lock of hair falling over his fore-head, to snuggle closer into his warmth, to lightly touch her mouth to his. To wait while wakefulness overtook him and events were allowed to flow wherever they willed.

Distantly, she remembered him carrying her to bed as the new day began. To lie in his arms had seemed the most natural thing in the world. They had drifted into sleep together even as the sun had crept over the windowsills and through the white lace curtains, sleeping as the day had aged. Now she guessed it to be late afternoon.

Carefully she rose, slipping from the bed so as not to disturb him. There was a second bathroom down the hall. There, she showered and put on the jeans and shirt she'd taken from the closet. With her hair tumbling uncombed around her shoulders, she went downstairs.

The horses were grazing contentedly in the paddock. In the yard in front of the house, several quick, darting blackbirds were pecking. Nothing moved on the road beyond. The world seemed wrapped in stillness.

She made a pot of coffee, then realized that she was hungry. There were cold cuts in the refrigerator. She got them out and began making sandwiches. She was cutting the last of them into sections when a sound made her turn.

Chas stood just inside the kitchen. He'd put his shirt back on, but left it unbuttoned. His hair was still rumpled and he looked slightly confused. "What time is it?"

"Almost 4:00 p.m.," she replied. "Want some coffee?"

He nodded quickly and lowered himself onto a stool at the counter. "I can't remember the last time I slept during the day. My head feels like cotton wool."

"Mine, too. Maybe some food will help. I made sandwiches."

He must have really been out of it because he looked glad about that. They sat at the table, eating and sipping coffee, while the fog of unaccustomed sleep lifted.

When they were done, Chas helped clear the table. He stood for a moment beside the sink, looking at Annalise. Quietly he said, "I'm going to do some work on the bunkhouse."

She nodded and began rinsing the dishes. The urge to go with him, be close to him, be touched by him was almost more than she could resist. When she heard the screen door close behind him, she closed her eyes and breathed deeply.

She needed good, serious work to distract her. Fortunately, where there were horses, there was never any lack of chores to be done. Wearing her oldest pair of boots, she headed out to the stables. In the distance, she could hear hammering. Chas was working on the bunkhouse roof. The rhythmic beat followed her into the shadowed coolness of the horse stalls.

She got busy mucking them out. There were people she knew in all parts of the horse business who hated mucking stalls. They looked down on the work and wouldn't do it under any circumstances, but Annalise found it oddly satisfying. There was something very simple and basic, yet also necessary, about providing an animal with a clean, healthy place to live. Besides, she loved the smell of fresh straw.

As she trundled the last wheelbarrowful away to be dumped far behind the stables where she did her composting, she glimpsed Chas still up on the roof. He looked as though he was almost done.

It was getting on for dusk. She led the horses back to the stables, made sure they had hay and water and got them bedded down. Chas was washing up when she came back into the house. She heard the shower on. Deciding to do the same, she used the shower in her room, then changed into a simple cotton dress.

When she came back downstairs, he was in the kitchen. The light had fully faded outside. A few whippoorwills chirruped softly but otherwise it was quiet.

His hair gleamed a dark gold, still damp from the shower. The sun had deepened the burnished glow of his skin. He was dressed in khakis and a white knit shirt that stretched over the hardened contours of his chest.

His eyes heated as they touched her. He moved slightly, as though to come toward her, then stopped himself. "Want to go into town?"

That surprised her. He didn't seem like the sort of man who needed to seek out company. But perhaps it was just as well. Staying home alone together presented all sorts of pitfalls.

"Sure," she said, "why not?"

They took his car. He drove well, the same as he did everything else. That could get tiresome after a while, say three or four hundred years.

The parking lot in front of the Pecos was filling up. They left the car, went inside and found a booth toward the back. A funny thing happened as they were making their way to it. Conversations seemed to break off, beer mugs froze in midair, people got really interested in the tops of their tables and even the music seemed to stumble just a bit.

"Offhand," Annalise said, "I'd guess folks aren't exactly overjoyed to see us."

Chas grinned. He seemed not at all concerned to have people clearly uncomfortable around him. "No such thing. They're just shy, that's all."

"Yeah, right, shy of getting in your way. You don't mind that, do you?"

"It's better than some fool like Fuller thinking he can mess with you."

"Like he *thinks* he can with me."

"Like he *thought*," Chas corrected gently. He broke off as a large, burly man came out from behind the bar and walked over to them. He had an oversize apron tied around his middle and a no-nonsense air.

"Evening, Annalise, Mr. Howell. What can I get for you?"

"Evening, Russ. Chas, this is Russ Padrone. He tends bar here."

Chas stood and held out a hand. The bartender hesitated a split second before taking it. "Annalise and I just stopped in for a little supper," Chas said.

Padrone nodded. He let go of Chas's hand, looked at him steadily for a moment and seemed to like what he saw. "I got a couple of nice steaks back in the kitchen. How about them?"

Chas glanced at Annalise. She didn't object. He nodded. "Sounds good, thanks. A couple of beers, too, if you wouldn't mind."

Padrone went off to see to both. The level of conversation returned to normal, but Annalise felt anything but. She shook her head silently.

"What's the matter?" Chas asked.

Her smile was rueful. "I feel like I'm in the wild West and I just walked into a saloon with a desperado. Everybody's sort of half-fascinated to see him, but they're also worried what he might do."

"What I'm going to do is eat a steak," Chas said. The beer came, brought by a young lady who couldn't seem to stop staring at Chas. She put his beer right down in front of him, but practically missed the table altogether when it came to Annalise's.

"I've got it," Annalise said, grabbing the mug just before it slid over into her lap.

The girl didn't reply. She seemed oblivious to anything other than Chas, even backing away several feet before she remembered to turn around.

"Give me a break," Annalise muttered.

"What's that?" His grin deepened.

"Just a comment on the idiocy of the female species." The band switched over to a slow number. Annalise put her mug down. She'd had it with being a one-woman audience for a town that seemed to have suddenly lost its wits. If that was how it had to be, at least she was going to have a little fun in the process. "Want to dance?" she asked.

He seemed surprised, but pleasantly so. Standing up, he reached for her hand.

Chapter 16

He couldn't remember the last time he'd danced. But the music was slow and undemanding, and anyway it was like riding a bicycle, wasn't it? Funny, though, he couldn't recall a woman in his arms ever feeling quite so good, her body moving lightly against his, her hands resting on his shoulders, all the rest of the world fading away.

They were alone on the dance floor. Distantly, he realized that was because of the way people were perceiving him, but it didn't matter. The notion of himself as some kind of wild West desperado was still amusing. And under the circumstances, it was probably all for the good.

Speaking of good, Annalise felt so warm and alive in his arms, so slender but strong, so completely feminine. Her hair smelled of lemon and sunshine. The little cotton dress she wore in a color that reminded him of honeysuckle did nothing to hide the curves of her body. He felt himself growing hard and tried to put a little distance between them, but she murmured something he couldn't catch and stayed close.

It took them both a moment to realize that the music had stopped. The band was taking a break. Awakening as though from a dream, they stared at each other abashedly.

Annalise's cheeks were flushed. She glanced toward their booth. "Our steaks are ready."

Chas followed her back, trying very hard to look at something besides the gentle sway of her bottom.

The food was good but Chas hardly tasted it. He couldn't seem to concentrate on anything except the curve of Annalise's cheek, the way her hair rippled along the back of her neck and the gentle swell of her breasts against the cotton dress.

Deep down inside, the saner part of him—whatever that might be—stirred impatiently. He was really losing it. Here he was, supposedly protecting her, when all he could think of was how much he wanted to take her to bed.

To make matters even worse, they'd already been there. She had slept in his arms as trustingly as a child. His body still held the memory of how hers had fit him so perfectly.

Padrone came back to see if they wanted another round. Chas shook his head. He didn't have a whole lot of hope of keeping it clear, but he had to at least try.

The music started up again. Several couples were out on the dance floor. People were getting used to the idea of him being there. The steaks finished, they joined them.

Time passed—an hour, perhaps more. He had no sense of it. There was only Annalise, warm and alive in his arms, and the music carrying them onward.

The crowd thickened. They became lost in it, once again anonymous. His head nestled in the curve of her shoulder, Chas breathed in the scent of sunlight and woman. His arms tightened around her. "Let's go."

She went without a word, hand in his, back out to the car and down the long, winding road to the house. Neither spoke. The night wrapped around them, screening out all doubts, thoughts, all worries. Tomorrow didn't exist. There was only now.

They'd left a light on in the front hallway. It illuminated their way up the steps. He'd lifted her, carrying her easily though for all her slenderness she was not a small woman. Strength flowed through him. He felt younger, renewed, almost reborn.

Her bedroom was in shadows. He set her down, but did not let go, his hands cupping her face, his mouth hard and hungry. He had meant to kiss her more gently, to coax her patiently, but the need she unleashed in him had an urgency beyond resisting.

Her hands fumbled with the buttons of his shirt. He covered her fingers with his own and looked deep into her eyes. "Annalise," he said huskily, "are you sure?"

She looked momentarily confused, as though the whole part of her mind that might reason this out was somehow disconnected. But then her eyes cleared, and with a faint smile, she nodded.

"Crazy, isn't it?" she murmured.

"Totally nuts," he agreed. Cool night air touched his chest.

In the movies, on television—and in certain books—lovers always got undressed quickly and easily. Clothing seemed to practically evaporate. Not in real life, though.

To start with, there were his boots. He tugged first one, then the other off, hopping on each foot. She laughed and fell back onto the edge of the bed, hair tumbling into her eyes. He brushed it aside and came down on top of her so that they were lying half on, half off the bed.

Her dress zipped down the back. Impatient, he went too fast and caught the fabric. Groaning, he tried again. In the end she had to help him, sliding the dress away from her shoulders. He did the rest, his big hands, the palms callused, slipping up under the skirt to caress her thighs. She was honey smooth, soft as velvet, heated to his touch.

Their mouths clung, tongues tasting. She made a soft sound, so piercingly female that for an instant he thought his control would shatter. He managed to hold on, but only precariously.

The snap on his khakis stuck. He muttered an expletive and wrenched it free. Her dress fell away, revealing high, firm breasts in a wisp of lace and the long, pale length of her waist. They twisted on the bed, torn between the need to do away with the barrier of their clothes and the equally frantic need to touch, to explore, to know one another in the most intimate sense.

But at last, skin touched skin all along the length of their bodies. Lying above her, feeling her warmth and strength along every inch of him, Chas twisted his hands in the pale nimbus of her hair and looked deep into her eyes.

"Annalise," he said, his voice grating, "are you absolutely sure?"

Had she said no, or even expressed the slightest doubt, he didn't know what he would have done, besides stopping, of course. Somehow he would have survived it, yet he couldn't deny the sigh of pure relief that escaped him when she took his face in her hands, touched her mouth to his and said fiercely, "Yes, I'm sure. What about you?"

"Oh, yes," he whispered, filled with a certainty and joy he had never before so much as glimpsed. His hands slid down her, molding her breasts to fit his palms, his thumbs raking lightly over the swollen nipples. She cried out softly and wrapped her thighs around him.

He kissed her throat, the scented hollow between her collarbones, the valley between her breasts, his mouth tracing a hot, hungry line down her middle to the dip of her navel and beyond the soft swell of her abdomen. All the while, she whispered his name with such mingled welcome and wonder that his passion was sent surging madly.

He raised his head, braced on his arms, the muscles corded, veins throbbing, and gazed down into her eyes. They were smoky with passion. His leg slipped between hers, opening her to him. Moving a hand over the soft nest of curls between her thighs, he touched the warm, moist center of her womanhood.

Touched and touched again, rubbing her lightly as the smoke swirled in her eyes, until her hips arched and she cried out convulsively.

Only then did he move between her legs, claiming her with strength and skill. She didn't hesitate, but received him fully. Yet he could feel how she had to stretch to hold him, heard the soft gasp of surprise as her body adjusted.

His teeth gritted. He held on by a shred of control, waiting, waiting, until at last he felt the rippling of her body drawing him further. Only then did he at last surrender to the molten need raging within him and thrust again and again into her until, in the incandescent merging of their bodies, it became impossible to say who was the possessor and who the possessed.

The release that came at last to them both was shattering. They lay slumped across the bed, still in each others arms, as the curtains billowed in the soft night wind and slowly, one by one, clouds drew across the stars.

Chapter 17

A truck coming up the road shortly before dawn woke Chas. Deeply asleep though he had been, a part of his brain remained alert to any sign of danger. He sat up quickly and walked, naked, to the window.

Billy Joe Jethro got out from behind the wheel, hitched up his pants and stood looking at the house. Chas pulled on his khakis and went down to greet him.

The sheriff spit into the dirt as he saw him coming. He took a hunk of chewing tobacco out of a pouch, added it to the chunk in his cheek and said, "Just thought I'd drop by and say hey."

"Kind of early for it," Chas said.

Jethro looked momentarily confused. "Guess so. I was just on my way home."

Chas didn't ask where from. He could smell the beer and moonshine, the cheap perfume and the tobacco.

An angry remark bubbled up in him, but he fought it down. A man could pick his own way to die.

"How's Fuller?"

Jethro made a sound that might have been a laugh. "Still madder than a rattlesnake in a frying pan." He peered at Chas. "His boys up and left, you know."

"No, I didn't, but I'm not surprised."

"Figured you wouldn't be. Still, that don't mean an end to it. He can always hire more."

"Think he will?"

Jethro considered that. He wasn't a stupid man, just a sloppy one. "Guess it would depend on how bad he wants Miz Annalise's land. From what I can tell, that's real bad indeed."

"But you've still got no idea why?"

"No, but I've been thinking on that ever since Annalise mentioned it. There must be a reason."

"I'd like to believe that," Chas said dryly. If a man was going to go to all the trouble Fuller had, it ought to be for more than a whim.

"Tyron Johannsen got by all right, but he sure wasn't what you'd call a rich man."

"That would be Uncle Tris?"

"Yeah, that's him. He knew this land like the back of his own hand. If there was anything especially worthwhile, he'd have done something about it years ago."

"Unless something changed," Chas murmured. He was thinking out loud.

"Don't see what could have." The sheriff gestured to the yard with its carefully planted trees to the rugged land beyond. "Things here are pretty much the way they've been for thousands of years, if not longer."

"Nothing much ever happens around here—is that it?"

"That's right. Storms blow through, droughts hit, but the land just doesn't change very much. Hell, even after that earthquake we had a couple years back, you couldn't really tell anything had happened."

"What earthquake?"

"Guess it didn't get much mention, but it was a big one by our standards, six point something on that— whatta-you-call-it scale?"

"Richter scale," Chas said slowly. "Six point something on the Richter scale. That's a pretty significant earthquake."

Jethro laughed. "Knocked every bottle off the shelves down at the Pecos. We were a week and more cleaning up down there and in all the stores."

"Was anybody hurt?"

He shook his head. "Nobody that I ever heard about. People got jolted out of bed, and were scared all right, but I guess we got kind of lucky. Not a single roof collapsed, no roads opened up. We did all right." There was a note of pride in his voice, communicating the fact that the people of Pecos had acquitted themselves well in a situation that others might not have been able to handle so calmly.

Chas believed him. For all that he despised Fuller, and thought Jethro himself was about the poorest excuse for a sheriff going, he found a certain quiet strength in the people who lived in such wild, open places. They were a special breed, set apart, and they knew it.

"If you come up with any ideas about what's got Fuller going, you'll tell me?" he asked.

Jethro nodded. He spit tobacco juice into the ground.

"Stuffs bad for you," Chas said.

"So's life. I don't suppose there's any chance you and Annalise are going to hotfoot it out of here?"

"'Fraid not."

"Didn't think so. Then I might as well tell you that Fuller's leaving for a few days. He's heading for Texas. My guess is he plans to line up some hands he figures will be a mite tougher than the crew he had."

"Think he'll succeed?"

"He's got a whole pile of money to throw around if he wants to.

"What I'm saying," Jethro went on, "is it might be a good idea for the two of you to take a little trip right about the time he gets back. Give this whole thing a chance to cool down. Whatta you say?"

"I'll think about it," Chas said, even though he was reasonably sure that Annalise wouldn't. Still, it wasn't the worst idea he'd ever heard. Maybe they could wait Fuller out, at least until they had some chance to discover what was motivating him.

"Thanks for dropping by," Chas said.

The sheriff nodded. He glanced toward the house. There was a look on his face, half wishfulness, half regret, all resignation. "She's a good woman. There's some you can't say that about."

A small pain flicked through Chas. He nodded. "That's the truth."

"I'm gonna take a chance and tell you something. Maybe Fuller ain't crazy and maybe he's got a real reason for wanting this land, but when it comes right down to it, that don't really matter. The fact is he is bone-deep mean and he hates to lose. For sure, you are going to have more trouble from him."

"I appreciate that," Chas said gravely. He hadn't figured on the rancher giving up after just a couple of setbacks, but neither did he particularly relish the worry in Jethro's voice. Clearly, even the sheriff thought the whole thing could turn out to be major-league bad.

"Comes all the way down to it," Jethro said slowly, "I'll do anything I can to help you. Presuming, of course, that there is anything."

"On the level?"

"Yeah, I guess." He laughed humorlessly. "Hell, I'm as surprised as you are, maybe more. As a general rule, I like to steer clear of trouble."

"What makes this an exception?" Chas asked even though he really didn't have to.

"Miz Annalise...she's always been real decent to people around here, hiring when she didn't really need to and helping to rebuild the church last year when we got hit by that twister. Not that I'm a churchgoing man... I'm not. I just thought that was nice of her."

"What about Fuller? Did he help out?"

"Him? You kidding? We had a little problem with drugs about six months back, stuff suddenly showing up in the parking lot behind the Pecos. Now I'm no tyro—there's plenty of drugs just for the asking—but people have had to go somewhere else to get them. We hadn't really been hit here, not until then. Make a long story short, turns out he was bankrolling the operation.''

"Is he still?"

"No," Jethro said quietly. "I told him there were limits. I didn't give a damn what he did somewhere else, but I drew the line in my own backyard. Anyways, he was kind of surprised, but he got the message and there's been nothing since."

"I see," Chas said slowly. He did, too. Jethro was like other men he'd met, disappointed by life and without much hope left, if any, but still possessed of a core decency that wouldn't be denied. Chas didn't really think the sheriff could be of much help even if push did come to shove, but he respected the man's dignity—what there was of it.

"I'll pass along what you said."

Jethro nodded. "Try to make her see it's for her own good. Fuller will find something else to fasten onto eventually. She's just got to wait him out."

"That might be harder than it sounds."

"There's a choice?"

"No," Chas admitted. "There isn't." He waited while the sheriff got back in his truck and drove away. When the dust had settled, he went back into the house to talk with Annalise.

Chapter 18

"I don't care what he said," Annalise insisted. "I'm not going anywhere."

"It's not a bad idea," Chas said. "If you'd just think about it."

"There's nothing to think about. Jethro's in Fuller's pocket. He's just telling us what he knows we're supposed to hear." She slammed a pan down on the stove. "I'd have to be crazy to listen to him."

Her mouth trembled. Abruptly, tears glistened in her eyes. She brushed them away impatiently.

Pain stabbed through Chas, pain for her obvious unhappiness, pain at the thought that it might not all be caused by Fuller. Did she regret what had happened between them?

He stood, arms hanging at his side, for a moment, unsure of what to do. Emotion of any kind had always unnerved him, undoubtedly because of what he'd had to deal with as a child. But he was a man now, a man who had lost a whole lot more than he'd won and who somewhere along the line had made a conscious decision to change that. Somewhere around Pecos, he suspected. Somewhere around her.

He put a hand on her shoulder. She stiffened, but didn't try to brush it away. Still, the tears slipped soundlessly down her cheeks. She wiped at them again, harder this time, as though she was angry at herself.

Chas groaned. Without further thought, operating strictly on instinct, he gathered her to him. At first she was unyielding, caught in her own pain and doubt. But that changed quickly. She relaxed against him, her head nestled in his shoulder, and sighed deeply.

"I wish we had met under different circumstances."

"So do I," he said and meant it. He wished they'd met on a sun-swept beach, far from every concern or danger. He wished he could pick her up there and then and whisk her away to such a place. He wished he were a different man, more willing to expect the best rather than the worst. He wished—

"But mainly I'm just glad we met at all."

She laughed, a soft, tremulous sound, and raised her head. Her eyes were wet, her cheeks pale. "Me, too," she said and touched her mouth lightly to his.

That tentative touch, demanding nothing, sent a bolt of pleasure through him so intense that he felt it to the core of his being. She did not regret, not him, not the night before. Here, in the harsh light of morning pouring over the plains, with all the worry pressing in on her, it was to him that she turned.

He ran a hand over her hair and stared in wonder into her face, feeling the stirrings of something he had never before experienced, except perhaps with Jimmy, and then so very differently. It shocked him that he could feel like this with a woman, on such a morning, in such a place.

"The bacon's burning," she said.

He hadn't noticed, but indeed it was. He took the pan off the fire as Annalise set the table. Over scrambled eggs and what he'd salvaged of the bacon, Chas said, "Jethro mentioned something about an earthquake a couple of years back. Were you here when it happened?"

She shook her head. "I was taking a filly to Kentucky. By the time I got back, everything was pretty much cleaned up."

"Your uncle say whether there'd been any damage?"

"I don't think so. The stores were the worst hit. They had all their stock on the floor."

"But here it was okay?"

She frowned. "Far as I know. Why do you ask?"

"No reason really. I'm probably just grabbing at straws. If it's okay with you, I'd like to take a look through Uncle Tris's records today."

"That's fine, but I have to warn you. They're all up in the attic and it's a mess. I'd better help."

First, they had to see to the horses. When they'd been watered and brushed down, they were let out into the paddocks. The day was warm; clouds were thickening across the sky. It looked as though it might be a good time to be working inside.

Annalise led the way up to the attic. The ceiling was high enough to let them stand comfortably. Boxes and trunks were piled everywhere. Chas saw an old dressmaker's dummy, sized for a woman with a generous figure, a bicycle with its front tire missing, an artificial Christmas tree still wearing a forlorn strand of tinsel. And far toward the back was the head of a moose glaring glassy-eyed at them.

"One of these days," Annalise said, "I'm going to clean up here."

"I wouldn't if I were you. Leave it to the next generation."

She shot him a startled look, but said nothing. Far back in the attic, where the light from the single bulb hardly reached, she bent down in front of several boxes.

"This is the stuff from the last few years. I guess we should start here."

Chas nodded. "Let's get it downstairs first."

Together, they carried several boxes down to the room Annalise used for an office. By the time they were done, both were sneezing.

"Uncle Tris saved just about everything," she said when she came back from getting a box of tissues. "He was a real pack rat."

"Good, maybe we'll get some clue to his dealings with Fuller."

"I'm not sure he had any dealings, but definitely he did not borrow money from him. There's just no way he would have done that."

"Did you look for any indication that he had?" Chas asked softly. He didn't completely discount the possibility that Fuller could be telling the truth. He just regarded it as extremely unlikely.

"I didn't go through everything in the strongbox. That's where Uncle Tris kept whatever he thought was really important—his will, life-insurance policy, bank books and the like. There was nothing to show he'd ever borrowed money from anyone, and certainly not from Fuller."

"Somehow he doesn't seem like the sort of man who would have tried to conceal a debt," Chas said thoughtfully. He'd never met Tyron Johannsen, but he had a sense of somehow knowing him, perhaps through the love his niece so obviously had for the deceased rancher, but also through the land, the horses, the devotion that had gone into both.

"If he'd owed anyone anything, he would have made sure it was taken care of," Annalise said. She snapped the twine on the first box and opened it. "If that's what you're expecting to find in here, you'll be disappointed."

"I'm not expecting anything," Chas said. He bent down beside the box and carefully lifted out the first few inches of papers. A quick glance showed that they were a mixture of bills for feed, letters from Annalise herself while she was away at college and what appeared to be a dance card from a social Tris had attended in the 1950s.

"Not big on organization, was he?"

"I guess not. Maybe we'd better start by making piles of everything."

They did so, working in companionable silence for more than an hour. The tiny details of a man's life emerged in foot-high stacks: bills over there, correspondence there, memorabilia like the dance card there and the biggest piles of all, miscellaneous.

"You're right," Chas said finally. "He was a true-blue pack rat."

Annalise smiled. "You should have seen what he did get rid of."

"Like what?"

"Old tack, finally, when it absolutely couldn't be used for anything anymore. Blankets that I swear the cavalry must have had. Some stuff that I never could figure out what it was for."

"But not anything written down or printed on paper," Chas said, looking around at the stacks. "That he kept."

A newspaper caught his eye. He picked it up and scanned the yellowing page quickly. "This is about that earthquake."

"Is it?" Annalise peered over his shoulder. The picture, spread across several columns, showed a grocery store, the aisles littered by fallen cans and boxes. "Doesn't look like there's anything there we didn't already know."

"I wonder why he held on to it."

"The excitement? It was a big event around here."

"I suppose," Chas said, but he was doubtful. Tyron didn't appear to have saved any other newspapers. Surely the earthquake wasn't the only worthy event that had ever happened thereabouts.

They spent several more hours going through the papers but try though they did, nothing turned up that seemed at all useful. Finally Annalise gave up. "I think we're barking up the wrong tree," she said.

Chas was tempted to agree with her. They took a break, sitting out on the porch and sipping lemonade. The sun had gone into hiding and there were thunderheads off on the horizon, but it was still pleasant to be outside.

Quietly Chas said, "Something occurred to me while we were going through all those papers. Your uncle was a careful man. Maybe he didn't put everything in neat files, but he had good records all the same. If there was something going on here involving Fuller, or something that could explain why Fuller wants this land, it seems odd that your uncle wouldn't have told you about it."

Annalise was silent for a long moment. Finally she said, "Maybe I'm reading too much into it, but the last weeks of Uncle Tris's life, I *did* have the feeling there was something on his mind."

"What was that time like? Were you here? Was anything in particular going on?"

She thought hard. "I was going back and forth to a couple of shows and delivering horses. The month before he died, I was probably away more than I was home. But when I was here, I did notice he seemed quiet."

"Was he ill?"

"His heart had been acting up for years. The doctor warned him to take it easier. When I was around,

I tended to fuss too much and he hated that so we tried to keep things as normal as possible."

"Then his heart just gave out?" Chas asked gently.

Annalise nodded. Grief swept across her finely drawn features. "I found him fully dressed lying down on his bed. He looked like he was sleeping."

"It sounds as though he didn't have much warning."

"I don't think he had any. He always insisted there was nothing really wrong with him and acted as though he believed that. My guess is he never knew what was happening."

"I wonder..."

"What?"

"If he didn't realize that he was running out of time, that would explain why he didn't leave any hint of what might be interesting Fuller. Maybe he just presumed he'd have time to deal with it, whatever *it* is."

"If *it* exists. There's still a possibility that we're looking for something that isn't there."

"That's true," Chas admitted. He finished his lemonade and sat looking out over the yard to where rosebushes bloomed up against the white fence. He'd been in a lot of places in his life, more than he could even remember, but he hadn't liked any place as much as he did this.

That surprised him. Generally, he sought the empty, wild places where other people didn't go, not a neat house with a neat yard and a woman who made him think about all sorts of possibilities.

A few drops of rain fell on the ground beyond the porch. They were followed by more. A sudden rush of cool, wet air banished the stillness of the day.

Annalise rose. She glanced at the sky and frowned. The thunderheads off in the distance were touched by the yellow-gray of serious weather. "I'd better get the horses in."

"*We'd* better," Chas corrected gently and was rewarded with a smile.

Chapter 19

"You're sure about this?" Chas asked. He wasn't taking any chances. Before he did what she wanted, he was going to be damn certain that she wasn't asking for more than she could handle.

"Absolutely," Annalise assured him. When he continued to look at her dubiously, she rolled her eyes. "Hey, if you're not up to it—"

"Who's not? Half a cup of pepper's fine with me."

"Yeah, you don't look like you think so."

"I'm telling you, it's fine. How much onion?"

"Three big ones."

He shook his head admiringly and went back to the chopping board. On the stove beside him, the chili simmered. "You weren't kidding. This stuff really will peel paint."

"Guaranteed. Also, if you ever get a bad cold, eat this and it'll kill all the germs."

"You're kidding?"

"No, I swear. It works every time."

Outside, rain lashed the windows, but the kitchen was snug and warm. The aroma of the chili competed with the fire crackling cheerfully in the old brick fireplace. Annalise paused in the act of laying another log on the fire. A deep surge of contentment washed through her. It was so powerful and so profound that it left her shaken. She had never felt like this, not even during the best days of her childhood. Her life was founded on self-sufficiency, especially since Uncle Tris's death. To suddenly find a man so necessary—and so welcome—confused and frightened her.

She closed her eyes for a moment, fighting against the contrary emotions that threatened to overwhelm her. When she opened them again, Chas was looking at her.

"Everything all right?" he asked.

She nodded. "Fine. Let me help with those onions."

Together they stood at the counter, chopping until both were in tears and laughing at the same time. Chas wet paper towels and gently wiped first Annalise's eyes, then his own. They covered the chili and went to sit by the fire.

Although it was only early afternoon, the sky outside was dark. "It feels almost like winter," Annalise said with a shiver.

Chas nodded and put his arm around her. It was done simply for comfort, but quickly enough the mood changed. Whether she turned toward him or he to her, it didn't matter. The fire leapt, hot and demanding. He said her name hungrily and drew her into his arms.

To make love with an extraordinary man in front of a roaring fire on a rain-swept day had always been one of Annalise's private fantasies. It wasn't particularly original, but she'd always enjoyed the thought of it nonetheless.

Now suddenly it became reality. The couch was too narrow and too awkward. He laid her gently on the rug in front of the fire and slowly, methodically, removed her clothes. When she tried to help, he stopped her.

"Lie still," he said softly. "Let me do it all."

Her eyes widened, but she didn't object. How could she when his every touch sent shards of pleasure through her? Her breath quickened and her heart beat beneath his questing hand. Submissiveness was not in her nature. To manage it required all her will. Yet there were rewards in the sudden, trembling passion his touch evoked, in the languor that swept over her, in the knowledge that he, too, was in the throes of desire as great as her own.

The skin was drawn tautly over his cheekbones. His eyes were shadowed, his mouth hard. He opened her blouse and spread the fabric apart, undoing the front clasp of her bra so that the lace fell open. Air heated by fire touched her breasts.

Reflexively, she raised her hands, needing to touch him in turn, but he caught them and stretched her arms out above her head, holding them there as he looked deep into her eyes.

"Lie still," he repeated. She subsided, astonished by her own obedience. This was something she had never known before, something at once playful and yet overwhelmingly potent. With a last flicker of hesitation, she surrendered to it.

Her nipples were already hard, but he didn't touch them. Instead, he undressed her, removing every stitch of her clothing and folding each article neatly beside them on the floor. When he was done, she was naked while he remained fully dressed. His only concession had been to undo the buttons of his shirt. He slipped a hand beneath her back and raised her so that her breasts rubbed against the fine down of hair on his chest.

Annalise cried out softly. Her hands clutched his shoulders. He loosened her fingers one by one and laid her back down on the rug. "Still," he reminded her as the corners of his mouth lifted.

His thumbs brushed the silken skin of her inner thighs, reached higher into the damp nest of curls that shielded her womanhood. Lightly he touched, stroking her until her hips arched and she cried out hoarsely. Holding her eyes with his, he spread her legs wide, then undid the zipper of his pants. She gasped as he freed himself.

Obedience was beyond her; there was only longing. She reached for him, guiding him into her. Joined, they moved as one until passion shattered and there was only blissful release.

* * *

"More?" Annalise asked as she lifted the ladle. Chas nodded. He grinned a little sheepishly. "I can't believe I'm eating this stuff, but it really is good."

She laughed and sat down again across the table from him. The fire between them was burning lower now but it was far from extinguished. The merest brush of his hands against hers was enough to remind her of the pleasure they had shared.

Hunger of another sort gripped her. She crumbled more salt crackers on top of the chili and dug in. It was raining harder than ever. Off in the distance, thunder rolled.

"Sounds like it's getting worse," Chas said.

"We can get some really bad ones this time of year."

"Let's hope this isn't one of them," he said.

They both glanced toward the windows. The rain was coming horizontally, so whipped was it by the wind. Although it wasn't yet sunset, the day was gone. Outside, there was only swirling, threatening darkness.

Chas got up. "Do the shutters work?"

"They should."

Together they went around the house securing the shutters. When that was done, it was much quieter, but they could still hear the storm battering the house.

"The horses . . ." Annalise said.

Chas nodded. "I'll go."

"No," she said with a smile, "*we* will."

Wearing rain slickers, they ran hand in hand across the yard to the stables. Falcon nickered softly when he saw them. Whatever Annalise had had to let go of in recent years as she managed the ranch alone, the stables hadn't been neglected. The horses were all snug and dry.

Chas refilled the water buckets while Annalise spread out more hay. She made sure all the lights were on before they left. Back at the house, they left the slickers to drip in the bathroom and changed into dry clothes. One thing led to another and it was some time before they pulled the covers over themselves, settling down, arms around each other, to sleep.

But not for long. A sudden flash of lightning illuminated the bedroom, waking them both. Hard on its heels came rolling thunder that seemed to go on endlessly. The storm, even more violent than they had thought, was on top of them.

Chas pulled on his pants as Annalise tried to light the lamps. Nothing happened. "The power's gone," she said, rising to dress.

"Do you have any lanterns?"

"Plenty, and I keep them filled." She took a flashlight from the table beside the bed and switched it on. They went downstairs to the pantry, where she kept the hurricane lamps. All the while, the storm raged. Annalise had always enjoyed dramatic weather, but now she winced. Each crack of thunder seemed to go right through her and the lightning was so bright that it burned her eyes.

Despite the shutters, they could hear the wind battering the house. Chas switched on the battery-powered radio and listened for a few moments. His face was grim when he came into the pantry.

"Seems the weather forecast was wrong. The storm was supposed to blow east, but it took a left hook and is hitting us instead."

"How bad is it supposed to be?" Annalise asked as she trimmed the wick on one of the lanterns.

"Bad," he said and went to help her.

This time, the rain slickers gave them scant protection. They were soaked when they reached the stables. The horses were pawing the ground in their stalls. Falcon's big body shook as he rammed against the door.

"Easy," Chas said, stroking the stallion's mane. "It's okay, boy. It'll be over soon."

But instead of winding down, the storm worsened. The stable walls creaked ominously and the lanterns they had hung from hooks swayed back and forth in the wind that got in through every crack.

The horses were somewhat reassured by the human presence, but even so their eyes rolled wildly and they stomped the ground. Annalise moved from stall to stall, stroking noses and doling out the carrots and apples she'd brought.

"This can't go on much longer," she said finally. Almost an hour had passed, yet the storm showed no sign of lessening. Her face was pale with strain and Chas didn't look much better.

"I should have brought the radio," he said. "If you'll be okay, I'll go back for it."

She nodded. "I'll be fine." With a gesture to the horses, she added, "I just can't leave them like this."

"I understand," he assured her and went out into the raging darkness.

Annalise dragged the stable door closed behind him and leaned against it wearily. She couldn't remember a storm this bad. Even when the winter snows came, the weather was gentler. Now it seemed as though nature itself had run amok, threatening everything in its path.

Grimly she went back to trying to calm the horses but her mind remained focused on Chas. She was counting off the minutes until he returned when suddenly, without warning, the sky split. A bolt of lightning struck so close to where she stood that Annalise was thrown to the ground. The air was filled with a tearing, shrieking sound. She smelled ozone and something else, something that terrified her as much as it did the panicking horses.

Fire.

Chapter 20

Chas was leaving the house when the lightning struck. Suddenly, night turned to a day so vivid that he instinctively shielded his eyes. The ground seemed to roll beneath his feet. He only just managed to keep his balance and hold on to the radio he was carrying.

When the glaring light died away enough for him to see, a ghostly nimbus seemed to hover near the stable, as though the air still reverberated with the energy let loose in it. Only once before in his life had he smelled ozone so intensely, during a similar lightning strike in the Philippines. Hard on it came another, even more ominous scent.

The lightning had split an oak tree between the stable and the house. The tree was burning. Even as he ran, the wind blew embers onto the stable roof.

He could hear the horses screaming. Their fear of fire was so great that in their terror, they would tear through walls, trample anything and anyone, and even run off the sides of cliffs to escape. Chas couldn't entirely blame them. The sound and stench of flames licking against wood caused a visceral reaction deep within him, too. He ran as he rarely had in his life and yanked the stable door open.

"Annalise!"

Dimly, amid the distorted shadows cast by the lanterns mercifully still hanging from the hooks but waving crazily in all directions, he saw her toward the fire end of the building. She was fighting the flames with a horse blanket, beating at them with all her strength. He joined her, but within moments he knew it was useless. Despite the rain, the building was too dry. The fire was a raging, devouring creature that could not be stopped. The only mercy lay in the distance of the stables from the house and barn. Even with the wind, they stood a good chance that only the single building would be lost.

"Quickly," he said, throwing down the blanket he'd been using. "We've got to get the horses out."

Eyes wide, face stained with smoke, she looked about to resist. But just then the fire leapt even higher than before, catching the beams of the ceiling.

At the same moment, Falcon threw his huge body against the stall door, cracking it wide. Chas reached him first and managed to yank the fragments of the door out of the way as the stallion surged past. Within seconds, the rest of the horses were freed and following him out into the wild, wind-torn night.

Annalise ran for the house to call for help. It came more quickly than Chas expected, a volunteer fire department made up of neighbors long accustomed to helping one another. They went to their business quickly but it was too late. Already the walls and the roof of the stables were falling in. All the fire fighters could do was douse the burning remnants.

The storm had largely blown itself out and dawn was coming as the fire fighters packed up their equipment and prepared to depart. Their captain came over to Annalise.

"I'm sorry, Miss Johannsen. We tried, but there was just no stopping it."

"I know," she said, her voice thick with unshed tears. "Thank you."

He nodded and went on. One by one, the trucks pulled away. Chas and Annalise were left alone beside the sodden ruin.

"We'd better start rounding up the horses," he said gently.

She nodded, but didn't move. Chas put an arm around her shoulders and drew her into the shelter of his body. That, at least, seemed to penetrate the frozen wall around her. She shuddered deeply. Against his chest, she said, "I'm not going to cry."

He caressed her hair gently. "It's not a sin."

"No, but I've done enough of it." She raised her head, her eyes meeting his. "Let's go get the horses."

Pride surged in him, for this woman and her courage, for her gentleness and her strength, for her refusal to indulge in even a moment's self-pity. Emotions tumbled through him—desire, affection, respect. And something that felt perilously like—

He pushed the thought aside. And not because it scared him to death. Absolutely not. There was simply no time to think of such things. Not now, and if his life continued on its usual course, not ever.

Except nothing had been "as usual" since the moment he'd pulled into the parking lot of the Pecos Bar and Grill and heard a woman scream.

The sky was brightening swiftly as they headed out on foot. Neither of their cars could handle the rugged terrain the horses could cover and there was no telling how long it would take to find even of the first of them. But after the long, wrenching night, fate turned in their favor.

They found two of the mares grazing peacefully only a short distance from the ranch house. Mounted, they were able to round up the rest within the hour, except for Falcon, who continued to elude them. When the mares were safely in the paddocks, Chas and Annalise set out to find him.

The day was aging—and their nerves fraying—before they finally heard the frantic whining toward the opening of the canyon they'd once explored together.

"Would he have gone in there?" Chas asked.

"It's possible," she said doubtfully. "But I'd think the confined space would frighten him."

"Maybe he was too scared to notice."

"If he's in there—" Annalise began. She didn't finish the thought. Grim-faced, they rode into the canyon.

They found Falcon a few hundred yards in. Sensing himself trapped in the canyon, he had tried to climb out, making it as far as a ledge partway up the south wall. Now, unable to go forward, he was afraid to back down and it was too high to jump. Spotting Chas and Annalise, his eyes rolled frantically and he screamed in fear.

"My God," Annalise whispered as she stared, dumbstruck, at the horse. "What are we going to do?"

Chas was wondering the same. He had never seen an animal get itself into such a predicament without actually being injured. That was the saving grace; Falcon appeared unharmed. But he wouldn't continue that way for long. At any moment, his fear would overwhelm him and he would jump.

"Easy, boy," Chas called. He dismounted as Annalise did the same. Handing her his reins, he said, "Stay here. Keep talking to him. I'm going up."

"You can't! If he bolts..."

Unspoken between them was the knowledge that if the big horse bolted on the narrow ledge, Chas would be knocked off and, at the very least, seriously injured.

"He won't," he insisted and headed for the ledge. It began only a few feet off the ground and tapered upward like a ramp. In fact, that was exactly what it seemed to be, a ramp rising along the canyon wall, crisscrossing back and forth to lead almost to the top of the canyon.

Curious, Chas thought, but there was no time to ponder nature's oddities. He went up quickly and reached the ledge within moments.

Below, Annalise was speaking soothingly, trying to hold Falcon's attention.

"It's all right, sweetheart. We'll get you down. Everything's going to be fine. Just don't move. Please don't move."

The words didn't matter but the tone of her voice did. It was filled with reassurance and confidence. Falcon still pawed the ground, but his big body trembled less and he had stopped whinnying.

Quickly Chas eased himself up onto the ledge. He pressed his back hard against the rock and inched forward, toward the horse's head. "Hi, boy," he said very softly. "You remember me. We had a great time together. But now you've gotten into a fix and I'm going to get you out. All you have to do is let me do it." As he talked, Chas laid a firm hand on the stallion's mane, his fingers tangling in it while the other hand stroked the animal.

Falcon's eyes rolled in alarm. He tried to toss his head. But the combination of Annalise's voice and Chas's rock-steady presence held panic at bay. Slowly, almost imperceptibly, the horse calmed.

"Okay," Chas called when he could feel the animal settling down. "I'm going to back him off."

Annalise paled, but she didn't object. They both knew there was no other way.

"Keep talking to him," Chas said.

She did so, repeating the same words she'd spoken before, over and over, a quiet, calming litany that didn't let up for an instant despite her fear. Chas slipped the bridle he'd brought over Falcon's head and tightened it. Holding the reins short, he pressed on the horse's massive chest.

"Back, boy," he said softly. "Trust me, we'll do it one step at a time."

The stallion resisted, refusing to take a step. His eyes rolled again.

"You're scared—I know that—but it's going to be fine. One step, just one." Again, Chas pressed.

The big horse shivered spasmodically, but he lifted a rear hoof. Hesitantly, all but consumed by fear, he stepped backward.

Chas resisted the urge to cheer and continued speaking softly. "That's it, you're doing great. Come on now, do it again. That's it . . . terrific."

All the while he was slowly, steadily backing Falcon off the ledge. It seemed to take forever, but in fact only a few minutes passed before horse and man reached the bottom. Chas let out a long sigh of relief as Annalise threw her arms around him.

"You did it, you actually did it!"

His smile was shaky but he, too, shared her joy. "Hey, give my friend here a little of the credit."

Falcon nickered softly and butted them both with his head. Annalise laughed and threw an arm around the horse. "You old fool," she said, "what did you think you were doing up there?" The tears she'd

managed to restrain when the stable burned would no
longer be denied. They trickled down her cheeks.

Chas caught one on the tip of his finger. He stared
for a moment at the gleaming diamond droplet. A low
groan escaped him. Horse, fire, loss, danger were all
forgotten as they clung to each other, shutting out the
world for however brief a time they could manage.

Chapter 21

Too soon, the world intruded. They got Falcon and the other horses back to the paddocks, and surveyed the destroyed stables again. Annalise went to call her insurance company while Chas put together a quick lunch. Neither of them had much appetite, but he thought they should eat.

She returned with some good news. "I'm covered for everything, thank heavens. An adjuster's coming out tomorrow. In the meantime, he said to go ahead and rent some loose stalls that can be trucked in and set up quickly. We should be okay by tonight." She looked at him apologetically. "I realize this isn't what you signed on for, but I really do appreciate your help. I could never have saved Falcon on my own."

He shrugged, embarrassed by her gratitude. "I got lucky. Come and eat."

They sat at the pine table in the kitchen. Outside, the sun was shining, the last of the storm blown far to the east. Except for the slightly acrid stench of burned wood wafting on the breeze, nothing remained of the fury that had raged all around them.

Chas leaned back in his chair. He seemed lost in thought.

"Penny for them," Annalise said.

"What's that? Oh, sorry, I was just thinking."

She flicked a smear of mayonnaise from the corner of her mouth with her tongue and smiled. "So I gathered. About how much easier it was in the sugar refinery?"

He laughed. "No way. Actually, I was thinking about Tris. Did he spend much time in the canyon?"

Annalise frowned. "Not that I know of. Why do you ask?"

"I'm not sure. It's a strange place—very remote, very beautiful. Is there any indication that it was ever inhabited?"

"I've never heard of any. As canyons go, it's pretty small. The Anasazi tended to choose bigger places, where more people could live together and they could grow food."

"I suppose . . . Still, did you get a good look at that ledge Falcon was on?"

"Good enough. I don't think I'll forget it to my dying day."

"I've been in a lot of places, and done a fair amount of climbing, but I can't remember ever seeing a natural stone ramp like that."

"What are you saying?"

"That maybe it isn't natural. I'd like to go back and take a closer look at it."

"If that's what you want to do." She sounded doubtful. "The stalls are going to be delivered soon. I can stay here and help get them up."

Chas shook his head. "No, that wouldn't be right. It's too big a job. I can check the ledge out some other time."

"You really think there's something to it?"

"Probably not," he admitted. "It just struck me as odd."

"If there were Anasazi in the canyon, I can't help but think it would be more obvious. They didn't conceal their settlements."

"Not usually, but they might have had reason to do so during times of trouble. At any rate, I admit it's a long shot."

"Still, we should look into it," she said. "It's just that there's so much else that needs to be done."

Chas agreed with her. Much as he would have liked to explore the canyon, the horses had to be seen to first. By the time the loose stalls were delivered and ready to be used, it was getting on for dusk. They were both exhausted and filthy. Under other circumstances, showering together would have been fun, but when the sole intent was to be clean again, they opted to go their separate ways.

Whatever amenities it lacked, the ranch house had plenty of hot water. Rubbing soap over his chest and arms, Chas let his thoughts drift. They didn't go far. He caught himself picturing Annalise in the shower down the hall and grimaced.

For a man who had steered clear of most entanglements, especially of the emotional variety, he was having a hell of time concentrating on anything other than her. The thought of her silken skin flushed and glistening provoked an immediate and unmistakable response in his own body. He groaned and briefly considered turning the shower to cold, but there was no reason to think that would have any effect and besides, he'd had enough shocks for one day.

He stepped out a few minutes later and toweled dry, only then realizing that he had forgotten to bring clean clothes in with him. His own were still in the guest room. Padding down the hall, holding the towel around his waist, he had almost reached the stairs when Annalise came out of her room. She had finished showering. Her hair hung in pale gold waves to her shoulders. She had put on a simple cotton dress with small blue flowers sprinkled against a pale peach background.

Catching sight of him, she flushed slightly. "Something wrong?"

He gestured toward the stairs. "I left my clothes down there."

"Would you like me to get them?"

"That's okay, I'll do it."

"Fine, I'll just put on some coffee. Or perhaps you'd rather have a drink?"

"Coffee's fine."

The hallway was narrow. He stood aside to let her go down the stairs. She did the same for him. Both hesitated.

"You first," each said.

They both started forward, jostled, backed off. Annalise laughed. Chas did the same. He was suddenly, vividly conscious of her eyes on him, moving over his bare chest and down his waist to the towel stretched taut over his lean hips and buttocks. Her cheeks warmed. She looked away hastily.

Coffee was forgotten. Clothes became irrelevant. He took a step forward. She touched a hand tentatively to his shoulder, her fingers lingering there to explore the hard curve of bone and sinew.

He drew a ragged breath. Her lips parted. The hall was deep in shadows, but he could see the grayish green depths of her eyes alight with shards of gold.

The day begun in horror and sorrow found its rest at last in the gentle quiet of her bedroom. But this time it was Annalise's turn to provoke and tease. With a smile that was pure delight, she took the towel from around his hips, laughing when he playfully pretended to fight her for it, and tossed it on the floor. The look on her face as she surveyed him made him close his eyes, struggling for control.

An instant later, he opened them in shock. Annalise's searching mouth drifted down his chest, her tongue tracing the whorls of soft hair, following the muscled contours of his ribs to the flat plane of his abdomen.

He sucked in his breath, his hands catching in her hair, as gracefully she slid to her knees in front of him. Her position was incredibly submissive but the effect was anything but. When she took him lightly into her hands, he trembled violently.

Pleasure mounted—hot, exquisite, almost beyond belief. His breath grew ragged, the blood thrumming in his ears. Their previous lovemaking had seemed to him the absolute height that lovers could ever reach. But he knew now that he had been mistaken.

With each renewal of their intimacy, they gained knowledge of each other. With each encounter, they became more perfectly attuned.

A low, husky growl broke from him. In another moment—

"Enough." And then, as he had never thought he would say to any woman—"Please."

An instant longer, she lingered. When she raised her head at last, her eyes were smoky with pleasure. Proudly, holding his gaze with hers, she undid the zipper down the back of her dress and let it drop to the floor. Standing before him, wearing only a wisp of lace panties, she said, "My pleasure."

Chas waited no longer. He gathered her into his arms and crossed the short distance to the bed. Laying her down, he lowered himself on top so that they touched along every inch of their bodies. A smile of pure male anticipation lit his eyes.

"My turn."

She made a small sound—half delight, half trepidation. Slowly, ignoring the driving need consuming him, he laved her nipples with his tongue, drawing each deep within his mouth. She cried out softly and tried to reach down between them, but he evaded her seeking touch and continued the hot, insistent pleasuring of this woman who was so swiftly becoming more to him than he could ever have believed.

Not until her head was tossing back and forth on the pillow, her hair spread out like a cloud over the fragrant linen, did he finally ease his thigh between hers and open her for him.

Even then, he hesitated, entering only the smallest distance before withdrawing. Again he thrust. Again he stopped.

She cried out, her hips arching. He gazed down into her eyes. "Look at me."

When she did, he thrust hard and deep. So exquisitely aroused was she that the secret inner muscles of her womanhood began to ripple around him at once. He groaned hoarsely, his control shattering at last, and felt the life pour from him on a vast surge of tenderness and hunger for the woman who held him strong and safe within her arms.

Chapter 22

Annalise woke to a sense of well-being that was all the more startling for no longer being novel. She lay for a few minutes, listening to Chas's quiet breathing and marveling over the fact that she was actually getting used to being with him.

Not that familiarity made the experience any the less enthralling. On the contrary, the better she got to know this strong, tender, proud man, the more difficult it was to imagine her life without him.

Her stomach twisted. She had never experienced this kind of vulnerability. It terrified her.

Quietly, so as not to wake him, she slipped from the bed. Downstairs, it was just beginning to get light. This was the time of day she liked best, when it seemed that the world was reborn.

Dressed in cutoff jeans and a sweater, she went to see to the horses. They welcomed her eagerly, none the worse for a night in unfamiliar stalls. She did the usual chores and let the animals out to graze.

Wind Dancer lingered, whinnying softly as she did when she wanted Annalise's attention.

"What's the matter, girl?" Rubbing her velvety nose, Annalise leaned her head against the horse's side and closed her eyes for a moment.

The clean, rich smell of the horse mingling with leather and hay surrounded her. The dark shadow that had lain over her since she woke eased a little.

"You know what we both need?" she murmured. "A nice, long run."

Wind Dancer tossed her head as though in agreement. Minutes later, the horse saddled, Annalise was about to mount when she suddenly hesitated. "I'll be right back," she said and ran into the house.

Quickly she scribbled a note for Chas, thinking all the while that she hadn't needed to worry about anyone missing her since Uncle Tris died. She wasn't at all sure how she felt about that changing.

Hurrying, she closed the door behind her and went to rejoin Wind Dancer. They rode out past the fence and turned west, away from the canyon, toward the high plain.

The breeze ruffled her hair. She pressed her heels into the mare's sides and urged her on, not that Wind Dancer needed much urging. She fairly leapt forward, covering the ground in long, powerful strides.

Annalise threw back her head and laughed. Behind her the sun was rising in glory. In front lay the new-born day. She could see for miles in all directions. Except for the road leading back to the ranch, there wasn't a sign of human habitation.

The nearest thing to it was a prairie-dog town nestled near the foothills. The town's early risers peered at her, standing upright, ears bristling and paws held like alert boxers preparing to duke it out with all comers. Still laughing, she waved as she rode past.

Always, she had loved to ride like this, wild and free, and alone. Sometimes her uncle had come with her, and occasionally a school friend, but more often than not she was content to strike out across the plain, a willing horse beneath her, and ride as one with the wind and the land.

It should have been the same this morning. The stable fire was over and done, the horses all safe and rebuilding to begin soon. Fuller had learned a harsh lesson and gone off to lick his wounds.

Despite his efforts, there were still a good number of horses coming in to be trained over the coming months. She could look forward to her business growing, her life getting back on track.

It should have been enough.

Yet even as Wind Dancer galloped tirelessly and the sun rose and the day warmed, even as the land spread out before her in perfect beauty, a sense of something missing gnawed at her.

At first it was very faint, so much so that she could almost ignore it. But not quite. It grew, slowly but steadily, until finally the sensation was unmistakable.

She was lonely.

That was absurd. Her own company should have been more than enough, given the loveliness of the ride and the day. She should have been completely content.

Instead, she was anything but. The dazzling sky, gleaming azure, merely served to remind her of Chas's eyes. The broad sweep of the land somehow recalled his own fondness for the wild and unspoiled. A small stream burbling up out of the ground made her think of when they had followed the river into the canyon. Wind Dancer herself brought back images of him helping her to fight the fire and free the horses. Images, too, of him risking his life to save Falcon.

Suddenly it was as though the day in all its glory barely existed. She had to fight the impulse to turn to him, as though he would automatically be there at her side, sharing the same delight in the ride in a way that needed only a smile or a glance to be communicated.

Sweet heaven, what was happening to her? She had known him only a handful of days and already she was imagining—what? That he would give up a life of wandering the world apparently doing pretty much as he pleased and suddenly decide to settle down in the back of beyond?

A green girl wouldn't be that stupid. Yet here she was, a hair's breadth away from fantasies about hearth and home, lives intertwining, a future built together. It was more than dumb. It was flat-out embarrassing.

She straightened her back and took a deep breath. Like it or not, the stranger who had come so suddenly into her life had upset all her careful, preconceived notions.

She had to start over from scratch, beginning with the hard thinking she should have done before admitting Chas Howell into her life and her bed. And her heart.

What did she really know about him? He had a son named Jimmy by a woman named Lisa, who was his former wife. Lisa was now married to someone named Mark. They lived in Michigan, where Chas had been visiting just before he came to Pecos.

Apart from that, he seemed content to merely wander. None of the jobs he'd mentioned could have required any real formal education. None required that he settle down, conform to rules, worry about the future.

She had to face it, he was what Uncle Tris would have called a rover, a species of male celebrated in song and story but not much use for including in any long-range plans.

And then there was that other part of him—the high, keening wind part—that had ripped her out of harm's way that night in the parking lot and then convinced Fuller's men they were up against an army they couldn't beat.

Somewhere in all that roving he'd learned a fair amount about violence, how to stop—and start—it.

Wind Dancer moved along more slowly, as though mindful of her mistress's thoughts. The sun was growing warmer, but Annalise hardly noticed. Hardly realizing that she did so, she pulled lightly on the reins so that they turned in a wide circle.

He said he had taken his son camping. Had his own father done the same for him at that age? Where had he grown up, and how? What had he hoped for, dreamt of, aspired to?

She wanted desperately to know as surely as she had yearned to feel him deep inside her only scant hours before. The physical closeness wasn't enough. She needed to understand him in the bone and sinew, the spirit and heart.

For what? So that she would ache even more when he was gone? Impatience gripped her and with it the shadow sense of impending loss.

Too much had been taken from her—her parents, her uncle, and now there was Fuller's threat to take the ranch. She would have to be the world's greatest fool to open herself to the pain Chas could so easily provoke simply by doing what he was undoubtedly best at—leaving.

It was all very well that he'd come to her rescue as he had and had stayed on to help out. But it would end eventually and he would be gone. She had to remember that, even if she couldn't remember anything else.

Her hands tightened on the reins. She shaded her eyes. The land spread out before her, endless and eternal. That was what counted, what could never be destroyed, not by Fuller or anyone else.

The land would always be there for her. Chas Howell was only passing through.

"He's wind," she whispered to the sun and the sky. "And I'm roots," she added to the land, truth and promise both.

The mare blew softly. They had come almost all the way back to the ranch. Annalise could see the neat fence surrounding the house, the paddocks and the barn. Where the stable had burned there was a scar on the land, but it would be gone soon. All would be as it had been.

No, not quite. She would never again be completely whole within herself. A piece of who and what she was would go with Chas when he left.

But not, she was determined, too big a piece. She would guard herself as well as she guarded the land.

Her head was high and her resolve firm as she passed through the gate again, bending down to close it carefully behind her.

Chapter 23

Chas frowned as he read Annalise's note. He'd found it stuck to the frig when he came downstairs. Considering that he'd expected to find her instead, it wasn't much of a consolation prize.

"Gone riding," the note said. "Back soon."

Brevity was all well and good, but surely that was carrying it to extremes? Wait, though. She thought to tack on the time. He glanced at the clock. She'd been gone over an hour.

"Wonderful," he muttered under his breath and tossed the note down on the counter. Waking alone in bed, reaching for her but encountering only emptiness, had not put him in the best of moods. He slammed around a bit as he made coffee, feeling foolish for doing it but not stopping, either.

He missed her. Well, so what? He missed lots of things—lazy afternoons on a certain terrace in the south of France overlooking the Mediterranean. Diving on the reefs near Sydney. A particular mountain in the Italian Alps that wasn't the highest climb he'd ever made but had given him the most satisfaction.

All right, they were things—places, objects—not people. He wasn't unaware of that. But he genuinely liked Lisa and Mark; he could almost be said to miss them. And he definitely missed Jimmy. All he had to do was think of his son to feel a yearning he realized would be with him for the rest of his life.

But Jimmy was a part of his life forever, as were Lisa and Mark. He had finally come to believe that, to accept it and give quiet thanks for all it represented.

Annalise was entirely different. She'd hired him to do a particular job. Granted, their relationship had swiftly gone much further, maybe too swiftly. He didn't kid himself. She hadn't married so far in her life because she liked her independence too much. There was no reason to think she would ever change her—

Married? He froze, staring at the coffee trickling into the pot. Maybe the smoke had gotten to him yesterday. Where in hell did he start thinking about marriage?

The one time he'd gone anywhere near that most serious of institutions, he'd created a disaster that rippled out to affect not only his own life, but Lisa's and their child's, as well. Since then he had scrupulously avoided the merest thought of marriage, except to be glad that Lisa and Mark's was so rock solid.

Marriage was for other people in a very different world than the one he occupied. He simply never considered it. Never.

Ever.

Okay, this once. But he wouldn't slip up again. He and Annalise had a very nice thing going. When it was over, it was over. They would go their separate ways, two grown-up, independent human beings with their own grown-up, independent agendas. Bye, so long, it's been great.

Yeah, right.

He sighed and reached for a coffee mug. He was thirty-five years old, had bummed around most of the world, known far more than his share of extremely appealing women, and yet here he was feeling like a kid in the throes of his first serious crush.

Except this wasn't kid stuff. It was rock-bottom serious.

Coffee, that was what he needed. Lots of hot, strong, kick-start-the-old-heart coffee. And work—hard, physical work that would let his mind switch off and his body wear out.

Let's see now... Yesterday he'd fought a fire, ridden several miles, rescued a horse off a rock ledge, ridden several more miles—surely a good day's work for any man. Except when all was said and done, he'd been able to think of nothing but Annalise. Yearn for nothing but her. As though she were air and water, and sweet life itself.

He filled the mug and swallowed a mouthful of coffee. It was scalding hot, but he barely noticed. All his thoughts were focused on the reality he saw rush-

ing at him with the speed and remorselessness of a lo-
comotive.

All this with Annalise was going to end and when it
did he was going to hurt. Badly.

Years ago, way down in New Guinea, he'd been
gored by a wild boar. He'd seen the animal coming at
him and realized with crystal clarity that he wasn't
going to be able to escape. In the few seconds that had
seemed to stretch out forever, an odd sort of acceptance had settled over him, almost a kind of numb-
ness.

That overwhelming feeling was happening again,
only in a different way. He knew how he was going to
feel and knew there was no hope of avoiding the pain.
But he could minimize it. Starting right now, he could
take a few sensible steps to keep from being gored any
more than he had to be.

He could, for instance, keep reminding himself that
this was all temporary and that he'd be a fool to think
anything else.

Coffee in hand, he went back upstairs, showered
and got dressed. When he came down again, Annalise was still out. He checked the time and headed for
the phone.

All that thinking about love and loss had reminded
him of exactly how he had awakened to both. Not in
the arms of a woman—much as he had a deep affection for Lisa, she had never touched him in that way.
No, it had taken a child to make him believe love was
real, that it actually existed, and that he could experience it.

The phone was on a long cord. He brought it with him over to the couch by the fire, sat down and punched in a long series of numbers. The call would be charged to his credit card. Eventually, the bill would land on the desk of his business manager. It would be paid promptly, as everything else in that aspect of his life was done.

It rang three times before a strong, male voice answered.

"How's it going?" Chas asked after he said hello.

"Pretty good," Mark answered. He sounded relaxed and content. But he'd been through his own share of tough times. He and Chas understood each other on a level neither had really experienced with any other male.

"Jimmy's still talking about your camping trip. He had a great time."

"So did I," Chas said, hearing the warmth in Mark's voice and glad of it. Lisa's husband was genuinely pleased that Jimmy had enjoyed himself. It would have been a mistake to say that he loved the little boy like his own son. Chas believed firmly that in every way that counted most, Jimmy *was* Mark's son. He'd never begrudged that before and he didn't now, but for the first time he caught himself wishing that he might someday know that perfect love and trust with a child.

"Is he up yet?" he asked.

"Just came down. Hold on a second."

Jimmy came on the phone, sounding sleep-rumpled but happy. "Where are you?" he asked.

"New Mexico. Know where that is?"

"Kind of. Whatcha doing?"

"Helping out someone. So you had a good time?"

"The best. When are you coming back?"

"Soon. You be good now and do what Mom and Dad tell you, okay?"

"I will," Jimmy promised. "When you're here next, can we go fishing?"

"You bet. You go get some breakfast. I need to talk to your dad again."

"Chas...?"

"Yeah, slugger?"

"You're my dad, too, you know. Mommy says so and so does Daddy. They say it's okay to have two dads."

His throat was suddenly tight. He took a quick breath. "As long as you're comfortable with that, it's great with me. You're a terrific guy. I'm really proud to be one of your dads."

"Thanks," Jimmy said with the simplicity only a child could manage.

"Let me talk to Mark again, okay?"

"You bet. Have fun down in New whatsit."

"New Mexico."

"Yeah, there. Love you. Bye."

Chas had a couple of seconds to get a grip on himself before Mark came back on the line. The other man spoke gently, as though he'd heard what Jimmy said and guessed the impact it would have.

"Chas?"

"Yeah, I'm here. He really did have a good time, didn't he?"

"The best."

"He's a great kid."

Mark laughed softly. There'd be no disagreement on that. "Absolutely, the best."

"Someday I have to tell you how glad I am that—" He broke off, not really able to go on. Fortunately, he didn't have to. Mark understood.

"So what are you up to down there?"

"This and that. I just wanted to give you a number, you know, in case Jimmy needs anything."

Mark jotted it down. They talked a few minutes longer. Lisa was in the final trimester of pregnancy and doing well. The baby was due in the summer.

"Jimmy says there's been a mistake," Mark said, laughing. "He asked for a puppy."

"Maybe you could name the baby King, or Spot, or something like that and he'd be satisfied."

"Good idea," Mark said, deadpan. "King's a little sexist, though. Maybe Spot if it's a boy and Fluffy if it's a girl."

"Fluffy's really sexist, plus it sounds like a cat."

"Okay, Spot if it's a boy or a girl."

"Works for me."

"But then you're hundreds of miles away," Mark pointed out.

"Hey, live dangerously. That's what I always say."

"About that . . . Everything okay down there?"

"It's fine. Why do you ask?"

"Experience. You don't usually settle down in places where nothing's happening."

"There's plenty going on here. I got up this morning, made coffee, decided what to wear, called Jimmy."

"I get the picture. You don't want to talk about it. Just take care of yourself, okay?"

Chas assured him that he would. He hung up a few moments later, thinking about the oddity of a man who had been alone for so much of his life having people who genuinely cared about him. That he also cared for them didn't strike him as odd at all. It merely seemed natural.

Something deep inside him that had been locked up for so long was finally breaking free. It had happened first with his son, and with Lisa and Mark. But that had merely signaled the thaw. Now the flood tide was upon him and he'd be damned if he had the slightest idea of what to do.

He didn't have long to think about it. Hoofbeats sounded in the yard. He got up and looked out the window. Annalise was back.

Suppressing the surge of gladness and relief that rose within him, he picked up his coffee, put his feet up on the table across from the television and switched on the morning news with the remote control.

By the time she came into the house, he looked as though he didn't have a care in the world.

But then why should he when he was just passing through?

Chapter 24

She was on a diving board extended out into space above a pool so far below that she could barely see it. The wind blew strongly, so much so that she feared she would fall before she could jump. A cloud moved in front of the sun. She was suddenly cold and wrapped her arms around herself, trying desperately to get warm.

The board shook beneath her feet. She swayed, gasped, reached out for something to hold on to, but there was nothing. Terror roared through her as she realized she was losing her balance.

The air was thick. She fell slowly, almost drifting toward the ground. Yet suddenly it was rushing up to meet her. The pool was gone; there were only rocks. Someone screamed. The sound tore the sky open and sent falcons circling high against the sun.

"Annalise!"

A voice, dark with worry, and a hand firm on her shoulder drew her back away from the rocks and the shattered sky. She gasped and struggled to sit up.

The dream let her go but only slowly. She was still half in it when she opened her eyes and found Chas crouching in front of her.

Immediately, she stiffened and fought to hide her fear. They had said little to each other since she came back. Both had seemed to seek tasks that would keep them apart. He'd gone out to work on the bunk-house, she'd stayed inside going over records. Or at least she had meant to. Events had caught up with her and she had fallen asleep in her chair.

And fallen into the dream. The reverberations of it still lingered. She felt cold and there was a sickness in her stomach, memory of the rocks waiting to destroy her.

"Are you all right?" Chas asked.

She nodded. "Fine. I'm just not used to sleeping at this time of day."

He took his hand away and stood up. "You screamed."

She closed her eyes for a moment, struggling for calm. "I'm sorry."

"There's no need to apologize."

They were being so formal with each other that she could hardly bear it. She stood up shakily, not look-ing at him. "What time is it?"

"After noon. Are you hungry?"

She shook her head. The last thing she wanted was food. Her head throbbed and she tasted bile in the back of her throat.

"The adjuster is due. I'd better get cleaned up."

Chas nodded and stood aside. She went upstairs quickly, aware of his eyes following her.

By the time she got out of the shower and was dressing again, a car had pulled up in front of the house. She fastened the last button on her shirt, tucked it into her jeans and hurried to answer the door. There was no sign of Chas. She supposed he was back at work on the bunkhouse.

The insurance adjuster was a young woman, in her twenties, firm but personable. She sighed when she saw the burned-out remains of the stables.

"You're my third call today. That storm leveled more air-to-ground lightning strikes in this area than we've had in five years."

"It was a doozy," Annalise agreed. She'd been a little nervous about dealing with the adjuster and was relieved to discover that there really weren't going to be any problems.

"I can write you out a check today," the young woman said. "Given what I can see here, we'll settle for the full amount under the policy."

Annalise nodded. She walked back to the young woman's car with her. On an impulse, she asked, "Would you like to come in for a cold drink?"

"Thanks. Ordinarily I would. But I've got four more stops to make today and then a ton of paperwork to get through." They chatted a few moments longer before the adjuster left. Annalise stood watching her car until it disappeared out of sight. She was reluctant to go back into the house alone, and impatient with herself for feeling that way.

It was ridiculous to avoid Chas simply because she'd faced up to a few hard truths about their relationship. She was a grown-up, after all, not some starry-eyed girl who couldn't admit when she'd made a mistake. Confronted by the danger Fuller represented, she'd let her emotions take control of her with predictable results. These things happened. She'd get over it.

In a hundred years or so.

Sighing, she glanced down at the check she held. It really was for a lot of money. Given the way her luck was running, maybe she ought to get it into the bank without delay.

She went out to the bunkhouse to tell Chas where she was going, only to find that he wasn't there. He was sitting a small distance away on a paddock railing, watching Falcon as the big horse ran, tossing his mane, giving every evidence of showing off for his audience. Chas, in turn, was smiling slightly. He looked as though he was enjoying himself.

Indeed, he looked oddly content sitting there in the late-afternoon sun, not at all the rover who was likely to pick up at any moment and go.

"The adjuster's left," Annalise said quietly.

He turned, but didn't get off the fence. "Everything work out all right?"

"Fine. I thought I'd go into town to deposit the check." She hesitated, remembering everything she'd thought about the need to pull back, to be cautious, to protect herself. A gust of sage-scented wind distracted her, making it hard to remember all her sensible intentions. Or maybe it was the light in his eyes that did that.

"Want to come?" she asked.

He slid off the railing. "Sure, why not?"

Heck, with enthusiasm like that, what was she worried about? They took his car. Neither spoke during the ride into town. The Shamrock Café was busy, cars in all the spots in front and the door swinging as people came and went. It was usually like that after a bad storm. Folks felt the natural urge to come together, reassure themselves that everyone was okay.

"I've got a few things to do," Chas said. He didn't suggest she tag along. "Suppose we meet back here in half an hour or so?"

That suited her fine. She had her own things to take care of, starting with the bank. The building was closed for the day, but the trusty old ATM was open for business. Minutes later, her account was a whole lot richer than it had been before.

That done, she tried to think what else needed doing. Strictly speaking, nothing. But she was damned if she'd show up at the Shamrock early and cool her heels waiting for him.

Instead, she dropped by the small pharmacy that had served Pecos for several generations and was still managing to hold on despite the big chains coming into the shopping malls. She picked up a few personal things she needed and spent five minutes or so going through the magazine and book racks.

Even so, she reached the Shamrock before Chas. Liz was behind the counter. She came over the minute she saw Annalise. "How's it going, honey?" the waitress asked. "Heard you had some bad trouble."

"The stables burned, but none of the horses were hurt. We'll get over it." *We'll?* That was wrong. She had to stop thinking that way. "*I'll* get over it," she corrected.

"Sure you will," Liz said. She put a menu in front of Annalise and poured her a cup of coffee. "Where's Tall, Blond and Handsome?"

"Around." Annalise pretended to concentrate on the menu. She still wasn't hungry, but she figured she ought to make the gesture. "How's the special?"

"If you like catfish, it's great. Well, hey, speak of the devil—"

The café door swung open yet again. Chas strolled in. He looked tough and serious, with a glint in his eyes that made several other men look away quickly.

"Get you something?" Liz suggested when he'd slid into the booth across from Annalise.

"Just coffee, thanks."

When they were alone, he arched his neck to get the kinks out and said, "Fuller's back."

"How do you know?"

"Jethro told me. I stopped by to see him."

"Did he come back alone?"

"Far as Billy Joe knows."

"That doesn't make sense," Annalise said. "Not if he really did go to hire more help. For sure he's got enough money, and with so many men looking for work—" She broke off, wondering what the rancher might be planning. "I suppose whoever he hired could be coming later."

"It's possible. On the other hand, what'd he have to go to Texas for to hire people anyway?"

"He's got contacts there. He does a lot of business in Dallas."

"How do you know that?" Chas asked.

She shrugged. "It's just common knowledge."

Liz brought the coffee. "Decided what you want, honey?" she asked Annalise.

"I'm not hungry after all. Thanks, though."

"You should eat something," Chas said.

"What about you?"

"I'm not hungry," he started to say, only to stop when his eyes met hers. Ruefully, he laughed. "Okay, we both eat—how's that?"

She nodded, suddenly happy for some reason she couldn't begin to identify. Liz grinned. She took their orders and went off, saying something about having the sense a gnat was born with.

Chapter 25

"I also asked Jethro some more about that earthquake," Chas said when they were finishing the b.l.t.'s they'd decided on.

Annalise frowned. He kept coming back to the quake and she had no idea why. "Did he say anything you didn't already know?"

"Not really, just that so far as he remembered the main damage had been concentrated outside of town. You know, Pecos was pretty close to the epicenter."

"Guess we got lucky then, all things considered."

"Guess so. A quake like that can cause deep fissures, trigger rock slides, cause all sorts of problems."

"That's true, but I still don't see why you're interested."

"Tris was," Chas pointed out. "He saved the news articles."

"He saved a lot of stuff, as you've seen. It doesn't necessarily mean anything."

"Maybe not, but I've got a feeling—" He broke off, lost in his own thoughts.

"About what?" Annalise urged softly. When he was really concentrating, his eyes turned a shade of blue that reminded her of deep, still water. And his forehead crinkled up just a little. And he had a habit of pressing the fingertips of his right hand against a flat surface as though that helped him think better. And—

She *had* to stop this. Just a few hours before, she'd convinced herself the smartest thing she could do was to get some distance from this man who threatened to swamp all her common sense and turn her emotions upside down. Being alert to every tiny change in him was hardly a good way to start.

"About the canyon," he said. "I still think there's something strange about that ledge Falcon went up. It just didn't look natural to me."

Annalise sighed and pushed back her plate. "Boy, once you get hold of something..."

His eyes crinkled up. "That's the truth."

The way he was looking at her made her flush. She wiped her fingers on the paper napkin and looked out the window. It was quiet, as usual. A couple of cars went by, but otherwise nothing stirred.

Usually the sameness didn't bother her. She drew strength from the predictable cycle of the days. But now, suddenly, it chaffed at her, mocking the turmoil of her own feelings. She needed to do something, to break the pattern, to take some control of what was happening to her.

"All right," she said before she could think better of it. "If you're so sure there's something in that canyon, let's go take a look."

"Now?" he asked.

She nodded, hoping she sounded a whole lot more confident than she felt. He was supposed to be helping her deal with Fuller. Anything that might get them closer to that—however remote—ought to be pursued.

Never mind that when Fuller was no longer a problem, there'd be no reason for Chas to hang around. She understood that perfectly well and was okay with it. That was just how things were. She could handle it. Really.

"It won't be dark for several hours yet," she said. "We should have plenty of time to check out the ledge."

Chas shot her a long, thoughtful look. He seemed on the verge of saying something. Whatever it was, though, he kept it to himself and signaled for a check.

The wind was blowing more strongly by the time they returned to the ranch. As they saddled Falcon and Wind Dancer, Annalise glanced at the sky. Chas caught her doing it and took a look for himself.

"Hardly a cloud in sight."

She nodded, reassured that the weather at least was working in their favor. As they rode out, the sun was slanting westward. A hawk circled lazily on the still warm air currents high above. The horses's powerful legs stretched out in long strides, covering the distance swiftly. Less than half an hour after leaving the ranch, they were approaching the entrance to the canyon.

The last time they had come this way it was in haste and fear, dreading what they might find. Now curiosity drove them. They drew rein near the canyon mouth and proceeded more slowly, following the course of the river. All around them, the canyon walls glowed in the late afternoon sun, streaked with ocher, violet and black.

"I wonder how long this river's run through here," Chas said.

"Long as I've ever heard. There are a few creeks and streams that have changed course in this century, but not this one."

"Then if someone had cared to live here, they would have had water."

"Not much else, though," Annalise said. She pointed to the narrow strips of sandy soil running along either side of the river. "There's almost no room for growing crops."

"Food could have been brought in, maybe stored here."

"Stored where?" She looked up, arching her neck to get the best possible view of the walls. "Have you ever seen Anasazi settlements?"

"Only in photographs."

A smile teased her mouth. "I can't believe it. Someplace you haven't been."

"I'll have to go take a look, but in the meantime, tell me about them?"

"They're very sophisticated, obviously the product of a well-organized culture. You can see how the cliff dwellings were built for shelter from the environment and also protection from other tribes. When you think about it, they were a pretty ingenious solution to all sorts of needs."

"Any idea how they were built, exactly?"

"The Anasazi took advantage of the relatively soft rock that makes up cliffs around here. They hollowed out spaces from natural fissures and small caves. By the time they were done, the major settlements had hundreds of rooms, housing thousands of people, all connected by ledges and ladders."

"In other words, they didn't make any attempt to conceal that people were living there."

"Exactly," she said. "Wherever the Anasazi went, they used the same form of construction. If they had come into this canyon, wouldn't we be able to tell immediately?"

"Not if only a few of them came," Chas countered. "Besides, they may have had a reason for concealing their presence."

"Such as?"

"Such as whatever it was that finally destroyed them. Maybe they were fleeing an enemy who had proved stronger than they could deal with. Or trying to escape disease. Or perhaps they'd exhausted the soil around the major settlements and were dispersing in an effort to survive. There could be any number of explanations."

"I suppose," Annalise said slowly. She was still far from convinced, but she had to admit that what he was suggesting made a certain amount of sense. After centuries of a flourishing culture, the Anasazi had come under enormous pressure that had ultimately destroyed them. The exact source of that pressure still wasn't known, but there were all sorts of theories. Chas's idea that a small group might have taken sanctuary in the canyon wasn't completely impossible.

"All right," she said. "Let's find that ledge."

They traced their steps farther into the canyon. As the walls narrowed around them, the wind whistled softly. It had a high, keening sound that sent a shiver down Annalise's back. She could almost imagine that voices lingered under that wind, whispering of ancient mysteries.

Halfway in they found the ledge. Sage bushes clustered near its base, partly concealing where it started upward from the level ground. There were still a few broken branches lying on the ground, mute evidence of Falcon's presence.

The horse nickered. Chas steadied him with a touch. "Easy, boy, you're not going anywhere near there again."

Together, they dismounted and let the horses graze. Chas approached the ledge, pushing aside the bushes so that he could get a good look at it.

"If this thing is natural," he said, "I'm the Tooth Fairy."

"You really think someone carved it?" Annalise asked. She had to admit the possibility was exciting.

"Come and take a look." As she bent closer, he said, "See here. It's almost the same width all the way up and there are no breaks. Even if some kind of natural phenomenon could split the rock like this, it wouldn't be so even for so many yards.''

His hand moved, hard and burnished, brushing aside the powdering of sand and soil that softened the contours of the rock. ''Look,'' he said excitedly. ''You can still see the marks here—and here—of a carving tool.''

Annalise leaned against him to get a better look. Her eyes widened. Although she hardly considered herself knowledgeable about such things, she had to admit that he seemed to be right. There were small, regular marks all along the stone that could easily have been made by a chisel of some sort.

Instinctively, she gazed upward along the length of the ledge, trying to imagine what it could have been like to kneel, hour after hour and day after day, patiently carving the stone like this. The effort was all but beyond her comprehension .

''It's incredible,'' she said softly.

Chas nodded. He was smiling broadly, delighted by their discovery. Taking her hand, he said, ''Let's see where it goes.''

Before she had a chance to reply, he started up the ledge, drawing her with him.

Chapter 26

Annalise froze. She was swept by an old, familiar fear—and with it, shame. "I can't," she murmured.

Either Chas didn't hear her or his thoughts were elsewhere. He continued up the ledge, still holding her hand. She dug her heels in and pulled back. Belatedly, he realized something was wrong.

"What's the matter?"

Her cheeks flamed. She couldn't meet his gaze. "I can't."

He frowned. "Can't what?"

"Go up there. I just can't."

"You're serious," he said, surprised. "I know some people don't like heights. But this isn't far."

"I know, but I can't." She was mumbling and hated herself for it, but she felt so unbearably stupid. Barely a few feet off the ground and she was acting as though she were suspended in space, out over that pool she had dreamed of.

"Hey, it's okay," he said softly.

She nodded miserably. "I'll wait down here. You go ahead."

"All right," he said, but he didn't let go of her hand. Instead, he closed the narrow distance between them so that he was standing directly in front of her. "But first, do you have any idea why you don't like heights? I mean, you can get on a horse where you're actually farther off the ground than you are right now. Is it just doing it alone you don't like?"

"I don't know. I've never thought about it. Horses are fine, heights are out—that's all."

He nodded, as though it made perfect sense when in fact she knew that it didn't make any. With a sigh, she said, "I'm not really sure what happened, but when I was about four, I climbed up on the bunkhouse roof. Uncle Tris saw me and was running to get me down, but it was too late. I fell off and broke my arm. Ever since then, I've stayed away from anything that involves climbing."

"Makes sense. What were you doing up on the roof in the first place?"

"I can't remember," she said and it was partly true. She didn't know for sure what combination of impulse and foolishness had caused her to climb onto the roof. But she did remember that she'd been angry.

Her parents had gone away again, leaving her with Tris. Much as she'd loved him, she'd resented their not being with her. Maybe that hurt inside her hadn't had anything to do with her accident and maybe it had. She'd never really know.

"Fear," Chas said softly, "can cripple us."

"So can a really nasty fall. I'll wait here."

"Suit yourself."

Still, he didn't move. Neither did she. His hand had loosened on hers. She could have drawn away, turned her back, stepped off the ledge. All she had to do was take that first step.

He seemed prepared to wait all day for her to do it. Tartly, she said, "I know what you're doing."

"What's that?"

"You're trying to convince me that there's nothing to be afraid of and I should climb the ledge."

"This isn't climbing. It's walking."

"To you, maybe. Not to me."

"Okay, it's climbing. I won't let you fall."

There it was, what she should have seen coming since the moment he suggested exploring the ledge. Climbing had nothing to do with it. It was all about trusting him. And herself. Trusting them both to do this thing together so that neither got hurt.

She thought of the dream, the terrifying plunge into emptiness, and realized she should have paid more attention to it. Her subconscious had practically been shouting at her, but she hadn't listened. This man was challenging her in all sorts of ways, upsetting every preconception she had and threatening to shatter even the illusion of security.

Her eyes met his. He looked rock steady, not unsympathetic, but absolutely sure that she would face no danger.

How could he possibly know, this rover who seemed to blow on the wind? How could she possibly trust him?

How could she not?

"I really am scared," she said faintly.

"I know. We can go as far as you want, or not at all."

"I'll never make it to the top."

"If you say so. How about one step?"

It seemed so silly, one step, so little to ask. "I can do that."

He took a step back, holding her hand, looking at her. She followed. One step. Anybody could do that.

"Want to try another?"

"It's silly, one step at a time."

"What's silly about that? It's how everything gets done."

She sighed, feeling foolish, but somehow not minding so much anymore. "Okay, one more step."

He smiled, as though she had accomplished a great feat. "That wasn't so bad, was it?"

"I'm still practically on the ground."

"What's your hurry?"

Despite herself, she smiled. "At this rate, the Anasazi could come and go again before I reached the top."

"Oh, well, then if you're in such a rush, how about two steps this time?"

Two steps. She could do that. One, two. Easy. She glanced over her shoulder. The ground was very close. They had hardly gone any distance.

"Two more?" he asked gently.

"You know I'm going to quit any minute."

"That's okay."

One step, two steps. Three steps, four. She glanced down again. They had reached the point where she was somewhat higher than she would be sitting on a horse.

"I think that's about it," she said.

He shrugged, looking not at all disappointed. "If you say so." Still, he held her hands.

"You can let go of me now."

"All right." He started to release her. The sudden removal of his warmth and strength, his nearness, was oddly more gripping than her fear of heights.

"Wait . . ." she said. Immediately, his hands tightened on hers again.

"Two more?" he asked and smiled gently.

They made it to the point where Falcon had stood, roughly as high as a third floor. Annalise was flatly astounded. She clung to Chas's hands and didn't look down, but she knew she was higher than she had ever been in her life.

"Well, what do you know?" she murmured.

He was grinning broadly, as though the triumph was his own. "I knew you could do it."

She laughed, pleased but still abashed. "It's not exactly the Matterhorn."

"Isn't it?"

She understood what he meant. For her to climb this high took as much of an effort—perhaps even more—as it would for an experienced climber to scale a mountain.

"There's a couple of tricks to this," he said helpfully. "First, I know it sounds like a cliché, but it's really a good idea not to look down until you've really gotten comfortable with climbing.''

"It's hard for me to imagine that day ever coming.''

"You may surprise yourself. At any rate, looking down undermines your sense of balance. Some people have a tendency to list in the direction that they're looking. They start to feel like they're going to fall because they really are leaning downward. So try to keep your eyes in the direction you want to go.''

"What else?'' she asked, telling herself that her curiosity was purely academic. She'd never actually need to know any of this.

"Keep a hand in contact with the surface of whatever it is you're climbing. Like this.'' Gently he let go of one of her hands and pressed the palm against the walls of the cliff. "Feel how solid that is. It's not going to suddenly dissolve under you or start to shake or anything like that. In fact, this is a very friendly cliff. I'd have to say it wants to be climbed.''

Her mouth twitched. She couldn't help it. Incredibly, given the circumstances, he was actually making her laugh. "That's silly.''

"Sure it is, but you wouldn't want to hurt its feelings, would you? I'm not suggesting you go all the way to the top, but how about just a little farther?''

The mere mention of trying to climb to the top was enough to start her shaking her head. But she stopped, considering. The stone felt warm to touch, warm and strong like Chas himself. Solid, and reassuring. Not at all threatening.

"Wouldn't you rather be looking for signs of the Anasazi instead of worrying about me?"

"I can do both," he assured her.

Together, step by step, they continued to climb. Annalise could feel the old fear shrieking at her, but the sound was very distant. Far stronger was her growing sense of elation and wonder, that she could dare to do what she had always believed impossible for her and have nothing terrible happen.

Realistically, she knew that if Chas were suddenly to disappear from that ledge, panic would overwhelm her. By herself, the climb was inconceivable. But with him, all things seemed possible.

She shut her eyes for a moment, fighting a wave of longing that was all but irresistible. Everything she had told herself during the early-morning ride came back with a vengeance. She had to be sensible. She couldn't wish for the moon. She had to protect herself.

"Look," Chas said suddenly, excitement lacing his voice.

Her eyes flew open. She stared ahead, up the winding ledge, to where he pointed.

"See that?" he asked. "The darker spot against the surface of the cliff?"

"A different kind of stone, mixed in with the rest?" Even as she asked, she knew that wasn't it. The way the sun hit the side of the cliff, something in the depth of a shadow, told her the darkness was not on the surface.

"It's an opening," Chas said. "Come on."

He seemed to momentarily forget Annalise's reluctance and truth be told, so did she. They climbed swiftly until they were standing directly in front of a narrow cleft in the cliff face.

"A fissure?" Chas wondered out loud.

Annalise slid her hand along the stone, never losing contact with it. Her fingers curved round, slipping into the cleft. Hardly a hand's span in, the opening widened suddenly.

"I think there's a bigger opening," she said.

"Can you stay here?" he asked, looking down at her. "By yourself, for just a moment?"

She hesitated. The thought terrified her. Instinctively, she started to look down only to stop when she remembered Chas's advise. Lifting her head, she pressed her lips hard together and nodded.

"You're sure?"

She managed a faint smile. "How long are you planning to be gone?"

"Not long," he promised. Turning sideways, he slid into the fissure. She heard his indrawn breath. Immediately, he reemerged. "You have to see this."

Holding his hand, she followed him into the wall of the cliff.

Chapter 27

"It's a cave," Chas said softly. They remained standing just beyond the entrance. The thin ray of light penetrating the fissure revealed a space carved out of the inner rock that was large enough for them to stand and move around in.

"I wonder how far back it goes," Annalise murmured. She had a sense that the shadows where the light could not reach were not the flat surfaces of walls, any more than they had been on the outside of the cliff. The space seemed to extend beyond the limits of their vision.

"We'd need a flashlight to explore," Chas said, "and unfortunately, I didn't bring one. But I don't think there's any doubt this was deliberately constructed, just like the rooms within the Anasazi's other settlements."

"It's much less obvious from the outside," Annalise remarked. "Almost as though it really was meant to be concealed."

Chas looked around slowly. He ran his hand over the interior wall, as though seeking knowledge from the rock itself. "There seems to be a basic conflict here."

"What do you mean?"

"The room itself is hidden behind the cleft in the stone that could easily be missed. But the ledge is in effect a ramp leading right to it. Why not rely on ladders to reach here and leave the cliff face untouched? That way, anyone who wasn't supposed to know this was here would have a much harder time finding it."

"Maybe it wasn't supposed to be hidden," Annalise suggested. "That's just our interpretation and we could be wrong."

Chas nodded slowly, but he appeared unconvinced. "The fissure could have been widened to make a more easily usable entrance and to admit more light and fresh air."

He looked around again. "It's hard to believe that anyone really intended to live here."

"Perhaps it was only too store things." The possibility was more exciting even than the thought that the Anasazi had lived in the room. They might be on the verge of discovering a trove of artifacts.

But Chas quickly dampened that hope. "Then why the obvious ledge? It just doesn't make sense."

"Is it possible that they simply goofed?"

"Sure, but is it likely? As you said, they were a very well organized and sophisticated society. If they went to all the trouble of building the ledge and chamber here in this secluded location where they didn't normally go, they must have had a good reason."

Annalise glanced toward the opening. The light was beginning to fade. Already, the shadows in the chamber were lengthening.

"It will be dark soon," she said.

Chas sighed. He was obviously torn between the desire to explore further and the realization that it simply wasn't possible. "I guess we can wait until morning," he said.

Together, they stepped back out through the fissure. As she did so, Annalise found herself staring out across the narrow defile to the opposite side of the canyon.

It was no great distance, but large enough to drive home to her that they had climbed higher than she'd thought. Forgetting herself, she instinctively looked down.

The winding course of the river seemed an impossible distance away. She gasped softly and backed up against the cliff wall. Instantly, Chas was beside her. He laid an arm gently around her shoulders and drew her close.

"Going down is the easy part," he said.

She closed her eyes, fighting for control. He was right, of course. She'd already done what she'd thought she would never be able to do. Getting her feet back onto the ground shouldn't be a problem at all.

Chas went first, holding her hand. He walked slowly but steadily. She followed the same way, careful not to glance over the side.

Even so, when they finally reached the bottom, her knees felt like jelly. She managed a shaky laugh. "I actually have to do that again tomorrow?"

"No," Chas said softly. "Only if you want to."

The message was clear—he wasn't going to try to talk her into anything she wasn't absolutely sure she was ready to do. She should have been grateful—and part of her was—but there was also a small, hidden part that vaguely resented his refusal to insist, or push, or in any way try to influence her.

Impatient with herself, and frankly bewildered by emotions she had never experienced before, she was glad of the diversion the horses offered. Mounted once again, they were starting out of the canyon when Annalise looked back up at the cliff.

Now that she knew exactly where it was, she could spot the darker rectangle that was the entrance to the hidden room. But it was remarkably well hidden. A thousand people, unaware of the room's existence, could have passed through the canyon without ever noticing the fissure.

Why then was the ramp so meticulously carved to lead right to it?

"It *is* strange," she said as the horses started forward.

Chas nodded. "Almost as though whoever did all this wanted the room found, but didn't want to make it too easy."

"Why would anyone do that?"

"I have no idea," he admitted. "But there has to be an explanation. There always is."

"And you still think it all has something to do with Fuller?"

"I don't see what else it could be."

They came out through the narrow opening and started across the open plain back toward the ranch. The sun was a red ball low on the horizon. To the east, a scattering of stars heralded the night.

They rode in silence, without the need for words, all the way back. By the time they dismounted in front of the temporary stalls, the sunset was beginning to fade.

"I'll get the horses settled," Annalise offered.

Chas nodded. "Spaghetti okay for dinner?"

She allowed as to how it was and they went their separate ways. As she unsaddled the horses and hung the tack away, Annalise caught herself wondering if she'd ever known another man who so easily accepted reversals in the ordinary male/female roles.

Uncle Tris had been as good a man as she'd ever known, but even he had thought the kitchen was more naturally woman's territory. Aside from chili, he'd pretty much left the cooking to her once she was old enough to handle it. Which had meant that they ate out a lot.

Not Chas. When she came into the house, he was in the kitchen, a towel wrapped around his lean waist and a large pot of water bubbling on the stove. The air was filled with the scent of garlic, onions and something she couldn't identify.

"Please," she said as she sniffed appreciatively, "don't tell me you're making the sauce from scratch?"

He shot her a chiding look. "Not unless you want to eat tomorrow. I'm just souping this stuff up."

"What are those green things?"

He groaned. "You're kidding."

"Basil leaves. I knew that."

"That's my girl. Want to set the table?"

Sure she wanted to—anything to distract her from the ridiculous shiver of pleasure that went down her back when he used that especially tender tone he did sometimes. My girl, indeed. She was a woman, not a girl, and she was strictly her own person.

She ought to say that, get it out in the open, clear the air. And she would have, really. But before she could, the spaghetti was done and they were sitting down to dinner.

Chas said something about the Anasazi, Annalise answered and soon they were talking, easily and naturally, one topic flowing into the other the way it did with people who knew each other so well that there was never any awkwardness.

The food was delicious, the conversation even better. She lost track of the time, of her hesitations and her doubts, of everything except the sheer pleasure of his company.

And the bittersweet admission that even knowing how high the price would be, she was coming to care for this man to the very fiber of her being.

By the time they finished eating, night had settled fully over the house and the land beyond. A cool breeze ruffled the curtains and the windows. On the wind came the night scents of soil still damp from the storm, prairie grass and sage, and the indefinable something that was the vast, empty spaces all around them.

Annalise insisted on clearing up; it seemed only fair after he had cooked. She took longer than she really needed to in washing and drying the dishes, stacking them back in the cabinets, wiping down the counters and the tables, the top of the stove. Everything she could think of to postpone the moment when she had to admit that she was done.

Yet it came all the same. She hung the towel she'd been using on a peg beside the sink and looked at the clock. It was far too early to go to bed.

She could claim she had paperwork to do and escape to her office but that was cowardly. The plain fact was that she both wanted to be with Chas and feared where it would lead. How many more achingly tender memories could she afford to accumulate before the burden of them became too much to bear?

Chas was in the main room of the ranch, a rambling space added on to several times over the generations with walls taken down and others built. The floor was wide planks held in place by pegs, the ceiling was crisscrossed by exposed beams and there was a large stone fireplace in one corner. Flames crackled gently.

He was stretched out on the couch with his feet propped up on a rough pine table in front of him. He appeared to be asleep.

Annalise stared in surprise. For a moment, she thought he might just be dozing, or even pretending. But the slow, deep movement of his chest convinced her otherwise.

It was all she could do not to laugh. All that time in the kitchen, all that worrying about what would happen between them. And here he was, fast asleep. If nothing else, that ought to dent her ego a bit.

With a sigh, she settled on the couch beside him and gazed into the fire. Vaguely, she thought that she would get up in just a little while and go get some work done. Much as she loved running her own business, there were always forms to be filled out, bills to be paid. She'd rest just a minute or two and then go—

Her eyes felt heavy. The lids drooped, opened, drooped again and this time stayed closed. Across the room, the fire leapt and outside beyond her grandmother's rosebushes, insects droned. Annalise heard none of it. She was lost in dreams.

Chapter 28

A soft sigh escaped her. Vaguely, she remembered being afraid in a dream—or was it in reality?—but this was different. She was wrapped in contentment, blissfully happy, and more than willing to stay exactly where she was.

Except that her leg was cramping. Grudgingly, she moved, hoping the discomfort would go away. It didn't. Despite her best efforts to resist, it drew her upward, out of dreams, back to consciousness.

She was lying on the couch. Her cheek was pillowed on Chas's chest. His arms were around her. The fire had died down. It was deep in the night.

With a low groan, she tried to sit up. Immediately, his arms tightened. He murmured something she couldn't make out and drew her closer.

For an instant, she struggled, trying to free herself. It was useless. His strength did not hurt her in the slightest, it simply held her immobile. Unless he decided otherwise, she wasn't going anywhere.

She closed her eyes, thinking the smartest thing to do might be to go back to sleep. But she was acutely, almost painfully awake. Every rise and fall of his breathing, every beat of his heart, every tiny shift or murmur compelled her attention.

She stirred again, trying to slip away. Again, she failed. Waking him didn't seem fair—or especially wise. Resigned, she tried once more to sleep.

This time, she almost succeeded. Instinctively, her body relaxed against his. She drifted on thoughts of Chas helping her to climb the ledge, standing with her in the stone room, at the stove. A smile touched her mouth.

"Sweet," a deep voice murmured.

Jerked out of her doze, she tried to sit up, but Chas had other ideas. He turned, slipping her under him so that she lay on the couch with him above her. Gently he traced her lips with a finger, lingering on the full lower one.

"Did I miss anything?" he asked.

"Miss—?" She was fully awake now, but still befuddled, a little dazed, her heart beating very rapidly all of a sudden.

"I didn't mean to flake out like that."

"You didn't . . . that is, it's only natural that you'd be tired."

"What time is it?"

"I don't know. . . . Late."

He glanced at the fire. She did the same. It was almost burned down. Only the embers still glowed.

His eyes met hers. He didn't move, made no attempt to get off her, yet neither did he do anything else. Almost impersonally, he said, "We should go to bed."

Her cheeks flushed. She felt the sudden heat, but could do nothing to control it. He saw, too, and laughed very gently. Yet his tone was serious as he said, "Remember what I told you about going back up the cliff?"

Eyes on his, she nodded. "It's my choice."

"So's this."

She could say no, get up, walk away and be done. Not for a moment did she doubt that he would let that happen.

He was a man of restraint and of honor. A man who could be trusted for all that the wind would call him again and he would go.

Her choice. Slowly she touched a hand to his hair. It was thick and warm beneath her touch. Her fingers twined in the curls at the nape of his neck. "You need a trim."

"I suppose I do, but I've got this thing about barbershops."

"We've got a very nice unisex hair salon I'm sure you'd like just fine."

He pretended to be dismayed. "Unisex here in Pecos? Isn't anything sacred anymore?"

"It's not actually in Pecos. You have to go five miles down the road to Rockford."

"That's a relief, but I've never gone five miles for a haircut in my life. Maybe you could do it for me?"

He raised himself a little farther so that she felt the sudden absence of him and passed a hand over his jaw thoughtfully. "I could do with a shave, too."

"I'm sure you can do that for yourself just fine," she said tartly.

"I'm sure I could, too, but I'll bet you've never shaved a man. You might enjoy it."

Her eyes gleamed. He was teasing and they both knew it. Part of her liked it, part of her didn't. "Only if I get to use a straight razor," she said.

He pretended to flinch. "That's asking an awful lot. Besides, I haven't got one. How about a nice double-edged safety?"

"Wimp city."

"Well, okay, if you'd rather I stayed scraggly." Before she could see it coming, he nestled his face into her throat.

Annalise yelped. "You feel like a steel-wool pad. Cut it out."

"Keep talking like that, woman, and you're going to turn my head."

"I'd like to do more than that. Come on. Stop."

"Only if you promise to give me a shave. What do you say?"

"I say you're crazy. Shave yourself."

She spoke firmly enough, but her heart just wasn't in it. This silly teasing undermined her defenses even better than straight-out passion would have. Somehow, she sensed he knew that.

"I'll tell you what," he said, very seriously as though this were high-level negotiation they were engaged in. "You give me a shave and I'll give you a back rub. How about it?"

She looked at him with wide-eyed innocence. "That's all?"

He sighed, like every put-upon male who had existed from the beginning of time. "Anyone ever tell you that you drive a hard bargain?"

"Fuller, though not in so many words."

"Forget him, he doesn't exist—not right now anyway. I'll tell you what I'll do—a back rub, and special this week only, the deluxe, European-style foot rub."

Now she really was interested, but as in any negotiations, it didn't pay to advertise that. "One foot?"

He looked heavenward, beseeching patience. "I'm going broke here. Just how much do you want for a shave?"

Everything, all of him, for all time. Wild horses couldn't have made her say it. "Both feet."

"One back, two feet?"

"Two's all I've got."

"Oh, all right, then . . . seeing as how it's only two. But I get shaved first."

That seemed fair somehow. She wasn't quite sure why, but then she'd have been hard-pressed to mention anything just then that she was sure of.

Except perhaps that he made her feel like no one ever had—passionate, exquisitely feminine, strong, yearning and slightly dizzy all at once.

Okay, more than slightly.

"Just one thing," Chas said as he got off the couch, drawing her up with him.

"What's that?"

"I always take a shower before I shave."

She had a sudden, flashing image of him naked and bronzed under glistening water. Her throat tightened. "I'll wait."

"How do I know you won't run out on the bargain?"

"Because this is my house and I have nowhere else to go?"

"Details. No, I think maybe you ought to join me. Save on hot water, cut down on soap consumption— it's the environmentally sound thing to do."

"Oh, well, I wouldn't want it to ever be said that I didn't do my part for the environment."

"That's the spirit," he said and led the way up the stairs as he had up the canyon wall.

Chapter 29

A soft groan escaped Annalise. They were standing in the shower under a downrush of hot water. Chas's hands were at her breasts, slick with soap, rubbing gently all the way to the aching nipples that were full and hard.

His thigh edged between hers, his manhood pressing hard against her abdomen. Her arms twined around his neck. Their mouths touched, parted, clung, tongues teasing, hot and hungry.

And all the while, the water poured over them both. She closed her eyes as waves of pleasure washed over her. Trembling, she reached for him.

He groaned deeply, and pressed her back against the wall, bending his head to suckle her. The sensation was so intense that she felt it to the center of her womb.

The muscles of his arms and back were corded with the force of his own hunger as he fought for control.

Lifting her slightly, he wrapped her legs around his waist and stroked his hands down the length of her back to cup her buttocks. "I wanted to go slow," he gasped.

"Later," she murmured, fingers tangling in his hair, trying desperately to bring him closer. "Slow is for later."

The laugh was a rumble deep in his chest. He put an arm firm under her bottom to hold her in place and stepped out of the shower. The floor was thickly carpeted. Laying her there, he braced himself above her and looked deep into her eyes.

His possession was swift and sure. She cried out once, not from any discomfort but from the sheer, astounding relief of it. Without him, she felt perilously empty, as though a vital piece of herself was missing. It was only like this, locked in the most intimate embrace with him, that she felt truly complete.

But there was no time to think of that. He thrust again, withdrawing, returning, the rhythm catching them. They moved as one, harder and faster, until too soon almost, release caught them both.

Gasping, they lay in a tangle of arms and legs on the floor, hearts racing. The smell of him—soap and sun, man and sex—filled her breath. Annalise stirred slowly. Her eyes widened as she felt him hardening within her again.

He raised his head, the skin stretched tautly over chiseled bones. It was not the face she had watched when he was asleep or seen across the table from her.

Passion controlled him, burning away the thin veneer of civilization and leaving only something far more ancient, primal even, that found its counterpart within herself.

Dazedly, he murmured, "I don't want to hurt you."

Through the heat of her own need, she heard his anguish and was moved by it. Softly she touched his face, tracing the line of his mouth and jaw. Far in the back of her mind, she thought ruefully that the night's growth of beard no longer troubled her. Indeed, its abrasiveness only heightened her arousal.

"You're not hurting," she whispered, surprised by how hard it was to get those few words out. Speech was almost beyond her. She moved instinctively, hips rocking.

He gasped, his head thrown back. Deep within her, he stroked, slowly, patiently, again and again, their bodies slick and hot, until her back arched and she cried out helplessly. Only then did he pour himself into her, crying her name.

"By all rights," Chas murmured, "I should be dead."

Annalise laughed softly. They were still lying on the bathroom floor. He was on his back, she on her side next to him. Lightly she touched a finger to his mouth, following its curve. "But happy?"

"Oh, yes," he assured her, "most definitely happy. Of course, I also seem to be about sixteen years old again but that could have its advantages."

"We should get up," she said reluctantly.

"No, I think I'll just stay here. All things considered, it's for the best."

"Silly," she said and rose, enjoying the sudden sense of being stronger than him, if only temporarily.

His eyes moved up the length of her, lingering on the cleft of her womanhood and her breasts. He sighed deeply. "Nature's ultimate joke. You bounce right up and I can't move."

"Bet you can."

"Bet I can't."

"There's chocolate ice cream in the freezer."

He groaned. "Satisfy one appetite and right away she's got another."

"Fine, then, I won't share it."

"The hell you won't," he said and got to his feet with the easy grace of a great cat.

Taken by surprise, she backed away. He started after her. She got the door open and darted down the hall to her bedroom. He followed.

Catching her, he held her tight within his arms, stroking her hair. With great tenderness, he said, "You are the most enthralling woman I've ever known."

To her dismay, tears stung her eyes. She looked away quickly. "Then you must really be into goose bumps because I've got them all over."

He smiled and let her go, but didn't take his eyes from her. She pulled on a robe and when he made no move to do the same, tossed him a pair of khakis. Softly she said, "You still need a shave."

Running a hand over his jaw, he nodded. "Sorry about that."

She didn't understand what he meant at first. He touched her throat, tracing the line of it down to the hollow between her breasts. "I've marked you."

She glanced at herself and saw that he was right, her fair skin was abraded red in places where his caresses had been most demanding. At the same instant, other sensations poured through her. She was swollen and tender between her legs, her nipples remained hard and aching, and merely standing so close to him, being so lightly touched, made her inner muscles clench.

"The light in the kitchen is best," she said and turned away, seeking the most deliberately unromantic place she could think of. Not that it would help much. She could be anywhere with this man, under any circumstances, and desire him.

She always would, long after the wind had carried him away again. Her hands shook. She looked at them, willing them to grow steady, and felt a small flicker of satisfaction when they obeyed.

Chapter 30

They ate the chocolate ice cream while seated at the kitchen table, spooning it out into big bowls until there was none left in the container.

"Now *this* is wicked," Chas said with a grin.

Annalise's raised her eyebrows. "You were thinking of something else?"

"Absolutely not. Chocolate ice cream, my favorite sin."

"Come on," she said skeptically.

He ladled another spoonful into his mouth. "No, really."

"With all the places you've been, I'd have thought you'd find one or two things you like better."

Chas shook his head. "Can't think of any."

"It's really your favorite?"

"Favorite sin," he corrected with a smile. His eyes were hooded as they swept over her. "There's plenty of other stuff that comes under a different heading."

"What's that?" she asked, aware that her voice was suddenly fainter. The man was making her ice cream melt, damn him.

"Necessities," he said and laughed when she blushed.

A short time later, Chas returned to the kitchen with a towel draped around his shoulders and dropped his shaving kit on the table. He sat down, stretched out his long legs and grinned.

"You're sure you want to do this?" Annalise asked.

"Not trying to chicken out, are you?"

"Me? You should be the one having second thoughts. But if you really want to take the chance of lifelong mutilation, hey, who am I to discourage you?"

"It's not that hard," he assured her. "Wet down, soap up, scrape off. Simple."

"Back and foot rubs?"

"That's the deal."

She approached him gingerly, not because she really expected to have any trouble with the shaving part of it, but simply because gingerly seemed a good way to be around anyone who could turn her life upside down so effortlessly.

He leaned back and closed his eyes, giving her unimpeded access to his face. Where to begin? It didn't seem right to just slop on the soap and hope for the best. He'd said something about wet.

She went over to the sink, ran a towel under hot water and wrung it out. As she laid it over his face, he sighed. The soap was the old-fashioned kind, a cake in a round china bowl. She got a cup of water, dipped the brush in it and lathered the bristles.

His face seemed wet enough when she took off the towel. Carefully she spread soap over his cheeks and jaw, then took hold of the safety razor.

"It's a new blade," he said, still without opening his eyes.

Oh, good, she'd probably inflict twice the number of nicks she otherwise would have.

"Which direction?" she asked.

He opened one eye and peered at her. "You've never seen a man shave?"

"I must have missed it. Sorry."

He looked thoughtful for a moment before settling back again. "Down."

Sounded simple enough. Slowly, hardly breathing, she drew the razor across his cheek. A swathe of clean skin appeared beneath it. There wasn't a nick in sight. She relaxed just a little and tried another. Success, more smooth, bristleless skin.

"This isn't so bad," she said.

"You're doing great."

Emboldened, she continued. The soap had a clean, citrus tang. "This is fun."

"Don't get carried away."

"No, really, I thought you'd be bleeding all over the place by now."

"Thanks for telling me that."

She applied more soap, really getting into it now, and went to work on the other cheek. Soon it, too, was gleaming. All that was left was a little on the jaw—

"Ouch."

"Oh, no, I'm sorry."

"It's okay," he said, sitting up, a finger pressed to the blossom of blood that had appeared suddenly along the hard line of his jaw.

"I didn't mean—"

"I know you didn't. Really, it's nothing."

Perhaps not, yet the sight of even so small an injury to him made her stomach clench. She dropped the razor onto the table. "I'll get a Band-Aid."

"It doesn't need that," he assured her. Glancing up, he saw her white face and frowned. "I cut myself shaving all the time. Everybody does."

When she was still unconvinced, he stood up and drew her gently against him. "Sweetheart, really, it's all right. My God, when I think of the things that have happened to me. This isn't worth noticing."

"I can't think of those things," she said, her voice muffled against his chest. She felt like the world's worst wimp, but she couldn't help it. The smallest hurt to him seemed of enormous consequence to her.

He ran a hand over his face. The light in his eyes was purely male. "My turn."

"I could take a rain check."

"It isn't raining."

"You know what I mean."

The back of his fingers caressed her cheek. His breath was warm against her. She felt the now-familiar melting deep within her and she trembled.

"Not here," he said and took her by the hand.

He drew the curtains in the bedroom, the ones they hadn't bothered with before, and left a single light on across the room from the bed. The covers were pulled back to the foot of the bed. It was very quiet.

"Lie down," he said.

"I could just sit up."

Chas smiled. "No, you couldn't."

Awkwardly, still wearing her robe, she stretched out on the bed facedown. Chas sat beside her. She couldn't see him but she could feel his hands as they slipped around her waist, undoing the belt and drawing the sides of the robe apart. Slowly he slid it from her shoulders and halfway down her arms, baring her back.

The air in the room was cool. She shivered slightly.

"Is there lotion in the bathroom?" he asked.

When she nodded, his weight lifted off the bed. Moments passed. She was lost in her thoughts, in the memory of passion still resonating within her, in the fear of emptiness to come.

The bed depressed again. He moved so silently that she hadn't realized he was returning. Cool, silken lotion touched her skin.

"Relax," he murmured.

She didn't think that could be possible but slowly, almost imperceptibly, the tension began to ease from her. His fingers pressed into her shoulders. A groan of pleasure escaped her.

"There's more," he said and proceeded to show her.

At some point, her robe fell to the floor. Annalise hardly noticed. From the top of her head to the bottom of the feet he attended to so thoroughly, she was consumed with sensation.

"Did you know," he said conversationally, "that the feet have more nerve endings than almost any other part of the body."

"No kidding?" So she could still talk; it just felt like she couldn't.

"Not only that, but Oriental acupuncturists believe the feet influence all the major organs. The base of the toes, for instance, right here on the fleshy part, are very important."

Another groan broke from her. She buried her head in the pillow and struggled to lie still. It was almost impossible. Her breasts were full and tender, and she was acutely conscious of the tingling between her legs.

"I'm not sure about this deal," she whispered.

"What was that?"

"Nothing."

"You have a beautiful back."

"Thanks."

"Terrific muscle definition."

"It's all that riding."

"Must be. Great skin tone, too."

The struggle to lie still beneath his touch was fast becoming intolerable. She gasped and tried to turn over.

"Chas..."

"I've never felt like this," he said thickly. She heard the astonishment in his voice and something more—

concern. It was all too easy to understand. She felt the same way herself.

He slipped down beside her and gathered her close. Dawn came before they slept.

Chapter 31

"Are you sure?" Chas asked. They were standing
at the foot of the cliff wall near the ledge. It was late
morning. Rising after only a few hours' sleep, they'd
eaten breakfast quickly and set out again to explore
the canyon room.

Each carried a flashlight with extra batteries. Annalise had also brought along a notebook. She hadn't
drawn in years but trusted that enough of it would
come back to her to allow her to sketch anything they
found.

"I'm sure," she said, staring up at the wall.
"Funny, it doesn't look as high as it did yesterday."

Chas didn't comment, but he did smile as he took
her hand and started up the ledge. Annalise followed
close behind. She was still careful not to look down

and she didn't pretend even to herself that she enjoyed what she was doing. But the stomach churning fear of the previous day had lessened, though by no means disappeared entirely.

They reached the fissure in the rock quickly and slipped into the hidden chamber. It was cooler inside, but darker than it had been during their first visit because the angle of the sun was different. Their hands were invisible in front of their faces.

Chas snapped his flashlight on and shone the beam around. A soft gasp escaped Annalise. It was larger than she had imagined, stretching far back into the cliff. She estimated that it was almost as large as the living room in her house or close to three hundred square feet. Yet there was no sign that it had ever been used as living quarters, no trace of wooden partitions or skin hangings, no interior walls. It looked as though it had been hollowed out and then promptly abandoned.

"I don't understand this," she murmured. "Considering what it must have taken to carve this chamber out of the rock, why does it look as though no one ever lived here?"

Chas continued to shine the beam in all directions. Quietly he said, "Maybe it was intended as something else—a storeroom perhaps."

Disappointment filled her. "Then someone must have discovered it before. There's nothing here." She brightened at a sudden thought. "Unless it's buried. We should check the floor and—"

"No," Chas said slowly, "I don't think so. If my guess is right, this chamber was always meant to be found."

"Why do you say that?"

"Because of the ledge. Anybody who had reason to think the Anasazi had been here, anybody who was seriously looking for something would have spotted that ledge pretty quickly and come up here."

"And been disappointed?"

"Maybe not just that. Look." He shone the beam in the direction of a dark rectangle standing out against the lighter stone toward the back of the room.

"It's another opening," Annalise said excitedly. She started forward, "Let's take a look—"

Chas gripped her hand. "Don't go rushing into anything. I've got a feeling—" He stepped in front of her and moved cautiously toward the opening. It was almost as narrow as the fissure that led from the outside but it wasn't as deep. Chas pointed the light into it. He leaned his head forward to look but stayed within the first chamber.

"I thought so—"

"What?" Annalise pressed against him. She couldn't see anything. He completely blocked her view.

"You're not real squeamish, are you?"

She flinched. "That depends. How bad is it?"

"Just some bones, old ones would be my guess." He stood aside to let her look.

Annalise peered around his shoulder. On the other side of the chamber, the ground suddenly dropped away. Anyone stepping through the passage without looking very carefully first would never have realized it until it was too late. Directly below was a pit perhaps ten feet deep. In the pit were the remnants of sharply pointed stakes and in among them, silent testimony to their effectiveness, were the dead white bones of at least one victim.

"It's a trap," Annalise said faintly.

Chas nodded. "Whoever was after the Anasazi and their treasure, they were in effect lured up here. Once in the chamber, they spotted the passage and went straight for it, only to never come out again."

"There's nothing but a blank wall on the other side."

"Clever," Chas said, "and deadly. If there were others, they must have gotten discouraged in a hell of a hurry."

"Maybe you've been right all along," Annalise said as they stepped away from the passage and its grim occupants. "Perhaps Fuller really does want this land because he thinks the Anasazi hid something here."

"Is it possible that your uncle found this chamber and inadvertently let that drop to Fuller?"

Annalise shook her head. "I don't think so."

"Tris must have known this land well. He might have spotted the ledge and followed it."

"Not anytime recently. He had bad arthritis for several years. There's no way he could have climbed up here."

Chas frowned. He shook his head slowly. "Then how did this whole thing get started and what's Fuller really after?"

"You left out one question," Annalise said.

"What's that?"

"How do we stop him?"

Unspoken between them was the awareness that they had to do exactly that. And that once they did there would be no further reason for Chas to remain.

They rode back to the ranch in silence. Chas helped unsaddle the horses and set them loose in the paddock; then he disappeared into the barn. He came back out carrying tools.

"I noticed there's a section of fence down in the north field. I'm going to fix it."

Annalise stared over his left shoulder and tried hard not to think how empty she was beginning to feel. "I thought I'd head into town and pick up a few things."

He nodded. She thought he wasn't going to say anything and started to turn away. But he surprised her. Softly, on air heavy with the breath of day, he said, "Don't be too long, all right?"

She smiled despite herself. Foolish though she knew she was being, it felt good to have someone caring about when she got back. He looked so good, too, standing there with the toolbox in his hands, his shirt hanging open to catch the breeze, a tall, powerful man setting off to do a hard but essential job.

"I'll pick up something for dinner," she said, lingering, watching him, even as what sense she had left told her to get in the car and just go.

She did, but reluctantly and with a conscious effort not to stare in the rearview mirror.

Chapter 32

The Shamrock Café was almost empty, most people being at work. Annalise took a seat at the counter. She wasn't really hungry, though she knew she ought to be. But she'd run her errands, such as they were, and she wasn't anxious to go back to the ranch quite so soon. She just needed a little more time to herself to try to get her balance back, or at least some part of it.

"What'll you have?" Liz asked.

"Coffee, I guess. How're you doing?"

The waitress gave her a long, level look. "Better than you. You look like you've seen a ghost."

Annalise had a quick, flashing image of the bones lying high up in the cliff. She flinched.

"Hey, I'm sorry," Liz said quickly. "I must have hit a nerve. What's wrong?"

"Nothing, really. I'm just tired."

"Have something more than coffee. An omelet, maybe?"

Actually, an omelet didn't sound bad. It came under the heading of comfort food, which was definitely what she needed.

Liz went off to place the order without a word about Chas. Annalise was grateful for that. With her thoughts in such confusion, he was just about the last thing she wanted to talk about.

Just about. There was other topic she was even less eager to pursue and it walked in the door just as her omelet was done.

"Well, hey there," Brad Fuller boomed. "How you doing, little lady?"

The man blew up her truck, sent goons to kidnap her and staged a commando raid on her ranch. And he thought they could exchange pleasantries.

"Go to hell," Annalise said and turned her back on him.

Dead silence, the kind that made the walls waggle. Blissfully, she didn't care. Let him sulk, let him explode, let him rant and rave. She was fed up with Brad Fuller and the problems he was causing her. She would especially never forgive him for being the catalyst that brought Chas into her life, only to have to face him leaving it again.

"Must be the wrong time of the month," Fuller said with a sneer.

Liz slammed the coffeepot down and took a quick step toward him. "Why you—"

"Forget it," Annalise said. "That's exactly the kind of stupid remark he'd make. What's the matter, Fuller? Trip to Texas didn't go like you expected? Maybe the good old boys over there aren't as stupid as you think."

Silence again. Liz was edging toward the silverware drawer, just in case she needed something sharp. Annalise took a sip of her coffee. A big part of her mind felt numb. She simply didn't care anymore. The anticipation of loss and pain were drowning out everything else.

Fuller smiled. Bad sign. Very bad.

He slid onto the stool next to her. Even worse.

"Get me a cup of coffee," he said to Liz, "and none of that slop from the bottom. Get it fresh."

"I'll give you fresh," Liz muttered, but she poured all the same. Strictly speaking, stupidity still wasn't grounds for being refused service.

"Fact is, I had a pretty good trip," Fuller said. He took a swallow of his coffee and nodded, as though confirming what he'd just said. "Pretty damn good, and you know why? 'Cause I learned a whole bunch of stuff I never knew before."

"That's great," Annalise murmured deadpan. "But I really don't need to hear about it."

"Yeah, I think you do. Besides, I've got a responsibility here. I always thought well of your uncle and I know he wouldn't like this situation one bit."

Annalise looked at him narrowly. Maybe the sun was getting to him. He wasn't making any sense at all. "What're you talking about?"

"You being shacked up with Chas Howell, that's what." Before she could say anything, he went on. "Heck, I know that kind of thing goes on all the time but this is different. No way would your uncle approve of your being involved with a lowlife like that. And the worst part is I hold myself partly to blame. Yes, I do," he went on quickly as though she'd been about to disagree with him. "I know I handled the whole thing about your land badly and that kind of pushed you in Howell's direction." Somberly, he shook his head. "I'll always regret that, I swear I will. But it's not too late to make amends."

"Give me the check, will you, Liz?" Annalise said.

The waitress nodded and started scribbling. Annalise reached for her wallet. No way was she going to sit there and listen to Fuller's nonsense.

"Hold on now," he said. "Before you run away, you better hear what I've got to tell you. It could save you a whole lot of grief."

"There's nothing you can say that I want to hear except goodbye."

"Oh, yeah? How about this? Shack up with a guy for his bucks and you'll end up earning every penny. I'd have thought you were a whole lot smarter than that, not to mention just plain better. But I guess I was wrong."

Annalise froze. Most of her knew she ought to get off the stool and walk out. But there was a tiny part that was unwillingly caught. What in hell was Fuller talking about?

"I've said it before and I'll say it again, you're crazy."

"No, I'm not, but there's plenty of people who'll tell you Chas Howell is. It runs in the family right along with all that money."

Liz's eyes were saucer wide. She stared from Annalise to him and back again. Silently she mouthed the words, What does he mean?

Annalise shook her head. She truly had no idea, but she was no longer thinking of leaving, either. There was a deep well of dread opening up in her that had to be dealt with. If there was anything to what Fuller was saying, she had to find out.

"All right," she said, "you're not going to be satisfied until you've spit it out so let's have it. What is it you think you found out about Chas?"

Fuller grinned. He settled back on the stool with the satisfied air of a man holding a straight flush. "Chas Howell, that's quite a name. You ever wonder about that? What kind of people name their kid Chas? Rich folks, that's who. Rich East Coast northerners with their apartments on Park Avenue and their houses in Connecticut, their private clubs and their Ivy League schools. People with serious money, the kind you can choke on."

He sighed expansively. "I got to hand it to you, you didn't sell yourself cheap. Problem is, you may have gotten more than you bargained on and that's what worries me."

He put on a sorrowful look so exaggerated that it was almost comic, and shook his head dolefully. "Any

man who would do what Chas Howell did to his poor
widowed mother has to be lower than low. I'll tell you,
you gotta draw the line somewhere. I've had dealings
with men who maybe weren't everything they ought to
be, people who weren't above shaving a contract or
bending a law. But I'd never have anything to do with
a man who'd do what he did."

He shook his head again more firmly and repeated,
"You gotta draw a line."

The tightness in the pit of her stomach was getting
worse. Annalise told herself she had to be nuts to believe a word Fuller said. Chas rich? That was crazy.
Look at the car he drove. Look at the way he lived.
Look at how hard he worked.

And that bit about the poor old widowed mother,
come on, that was straight out of a Grade B movie.
Still, Fuller looked awfully pleased with himself.

"It's possible I'm having a bad day," Annalise said,
"but I don't get a word you're saying."

"I don't blame you," Fuller replied. "I wouldn't
want to get it either if I was in your shoes. But here it
is in a nutshell. Chas Howell's got himself a mighty
nasty reputation. He grew up richer than you can
imagine and figured he ought to have everything his
own way. Now that's not so unusual under the circumstances, but he went one better. First chance he
got, he had his widowed mother committed. I'm not
kidding. He went the whole nine yards—cooperative
judge, court order, the whole bit. Slam-dunked her
straight into a genuine institution and waltzed off with
full control of all the family money. She's still there

and he's free as a bird. Lives a real bizarre life, wandering all over the world. Been involved in all kinds of things. There's been rumors about him walking out on his wife, trying to kidnap their kid—all sorts of things. But anyway, the point is whatever he's promised you, you better not be counting on him. He's got a way of using people to his own ends.''

Chas rich? She was still stuck on that one, trying to get past a possibility that simply didn't agree with anything she thought she knew about him. Then there was all that other stuff—mother, committed, wife, *trying to kidnap their son*. That would have to be Jimmy whom he spoke of so lovingly and who he'd been to visit just before coming to Pecos.

"You've got the wrong guy," she said firmly.

Fuller sighed. "I just knew you'd say that. The trouble is, you can't tell your friends from your enemies. I've known you all your life and I just want what's right for you."

"You've got to be kidding—"

He held up a hand placatingly. "Okay, I made one or two wrong moves. But we can sort all that out. I just don't see how you can trust a man like that who's done the kind of things he has to other people."

"But you think I can trust *you?*" Annalise asked incredulously. For sure, he'd been out in the sun too long.

"I admit I was clumsy. But if you'd just gone with my boys the other night, we would have had a nice talk and gotten everything straightened out. Nobody would have gotten hurt. Instead, Howell comes along,

I got two boys basically crippled and all of a sudden you're off and running with Rambo. You got any idea how that looks?''

"I'd say it looks like you've been hitting the cactus juice. Those good old boys of yours are a couple of goons. They were lucky to get off as lightly as they did."

"Now see, that's just what I'm talking about. You've got this attitude problem and it's all because of the hogwash he's been feeding you. Next thing you're involved in some big-deal shoot-out at your place. Whatta you want to get into that kind of trouble for? I mean, I'm all for guns, but Howell looks to be into a whole lot more serious stuff than that. The man is flat-out dangerous."

Annalise thought of the firecrackers and the non-Molotov cocktails. She started feeling a little better but not much. Maybe Fuller wasn't totally off base about Chas, but he had raised a few questions she couldn't answer. All along she'd known that Chas wasn't being exactly forthcoming with her, but she'd never suspected how much he was concealing. If there was anything to what Fuller was saying, Chas had left out a whole lot more than he'd said. Like a lifetime's worth.

And that thing about his mother... She could discount the part about Jimmy. It just didn't jive with the way Chas spoke of him, or of Mark and Lisa. But his mother? He'd never even mentioned having a mother, much less having problems with her.

But then he hadn't mentioned all that money, either. He'd let her go along thinking he was a rover, wandering from job to job with no more than a few bucks in his pocket and no real prospects.

Fuller had to be wrong. He simply had to be.

"I've got to go," she said and slid off the stool.

"Right now? I was hoping we could have a little chat."

"We've had it. I'm not selling my land and that's final. If you honestly believe you've got a right to it, take me to court."

The rancher's face darkened. "You're making a mistake," he warned.

"Am I?" She hesitated, thinking she really ought to just go. But instead, she said, "You've got something driving you, something that makes you want my land so bad you're willing to do just about anything to get it. Chas has a theory why that is and I think he might be right. So I'm going to tell you this. If it's the Anasazi you're interested in, we did find evidence of them in the canyon on my property. We also found a dead body that belonged to the last guy who went snooping around them. He didn't get anything for his trouble and neither will you, so just back off. Understand?"

Maybe he did and maybe he didn't. Whichever was the case, Fuller was staring at her with his mouth open and a look of blank astonishment in his eyes. "The Anasazi—"

"Left bones and nothing else. Whatever you thought was in the canyon isn't."

She paid the check and pocketed her wallet. Fuller didn't move. He sat there staring at her, holding the coffee mug so tightly that his knuckles shone white. Some of the steaming hot liquid splashed on his hand. He didn't notice.

Annalise walked out into the sunlight. She stood for a minute, trying to decide what to do. Pride and simple honesty didn't leave a whole lot of choice. She got back in the car and headed for the ranch.

Chas was still working on the fence when she pulled up. She could see him off in the distance. He'd stripped off his shirt. The sun gleamed on his skin and on the bunched muscles of his shoulders and back. He swung a mallet over his head, driving in a new post, then repeated the motion. Each blow was rhythmic, graceful, seemingly effortless. He looked like a man content with himself and his task.

She walked toward him. He caught sight of her out of the corner of his eye and stopped, turning to look at her. He was just starting to smile when she stopped where she was and said, "We've got to talk."

Chapter 33

"A funny thing happened," Annalise said.

Chas set the mallet down. He wiped the sleeve of his shirt across his forehead. "What was that?"

"I ran into Fuller."

He stiffened. "Did he give you any trouble?"

"Not the way you mean. He was telling me about his trip to Texas."

His brows drew together. She sensed the growing caution in him and knew that he was a jump ahead of her. A shudder seemed to snap into place deep within his eyes.

"Busy was he?"

"Seems that way. He came home with a humdinger of a story, all about you being raised rich back East, walking out on your wife, trying to kidnap your son and oh, yes, something about getting your poor old widowed mother committed so you could take over all the family money. Quite a tale, isn't it?''

"Sounds like it."

"Any of it true?" She held her breath, not looking at him. Just let him say *Hell, no, you must be crazy to even ask that. Sure I broke up with Lisa, but as for the rest of it, what a crock.* Please, just let him say that.

"Most of it."

Her stomach twisted. She put a hand to it and fought to keep from bending over double. The worst passed in a moment, leaving her feeling blessedly numb.

"What part isn't?" she asked.

"Trying to kidnap Jimmy. It was my mother that did that. I just stopped her."

His mother had tried to kidnap his son? Sweet heaven, what kind of family was this?

"You're kidding?"

He gave her a pained smile. "'Fraid not."

"And you never saw fit to mention any of this?"

Chas shrugged. He leaned against the fence, crossed his arms over his broad chest and stared at her. "It didn't seem important."

He was serious. He actually thought he could all but take over her life without telling her any of the most important things that had happened in his. The message couldn't have been clearer. Why should he open up to her, reveal his true self with all the risk that involved, when he was only passing through?

"The money...?" she asked, feeling as though she was going to choke.

"It's always been there. I don't think about it much."

Oh, he didn't? How nice for him. She remembered scraping and scheming to put together enough to keep the horses fed, lying awake at night trying to figure which bills could be paid right away and which had to wait, breaking out in a cold sweat thinking that she would never be able to manage.

Things were better now, but money was still tight. It was for basically everyone except the rich. They lived in a world she couldn't begin to imagine.

"I guess this has all been a big joke to you."

His expression was unreadable. "Is that what you think?"

"What else could I? You tell me almost nothing, leave me to find it out from Fuller of all people, and you still expect me to trust you? How can I possibly?"

There was still a chance he could say something that would explain it all, make it all better. Not much of one, to be sure, but still a chance.

"I guess that's up to you," he said and picked up the mallet again.

Damn him, damn him, damn him. Damn his six ways to Sunday and every way in between. Tears stinging her eyes, Annalise walked, not ran—pride held out that much—back to the house. But she didn't go inside. The thought of being alone there, with far too many memories, stopped her.

Standing on the porch, she glanced at the sky. There were still several hours of daylight left. She could go for a ride.

Wind Dancer came at her whistle. "Good girl," Annalise murmured. Her voice broke. The horse nickered softly and turned her head to butt against her. "Let's get out of here," Annalise said and tossed the saddle on.

She had no particular direction in mind. Her only thought was to put as much distance as she realistically could between herself and the pain that was already growing unbearable. Without thought, she turned the mare in the direction of the canyon.

Chas put down the mallet and leaned against it. He stared, unseeing, into space. A black hole seemed to have opened up inside him. He felt as though he were falling into it and had no idea of how to stop.

Sweet Lord, this hurt. The look on her face when she said that she could never trust him had felt like a knife going straight through his heart. It was crazy, it was anguishing. It was terrifying.

Worst of all, she was right. Why should she trust him when he hadn't been straight with her about much of anything? Not about his past, his feelings, his hopes.

Did he have hopes? He hadn't used to think so. Hopes implied a future and he'd never thought about that much except in so far as it involved Jimmy. And

Lisa and Mark. And their new baby. He had hopes for all of them. But for himself, there had been an absence he hadn't been aware of until now.

He'd blown it really badly. That much he knew without anyone having to tell him. Her face had said it all.

He could try to explain, but that would mean opening it all up—the shame and fear, the pain of a small child and the rage of a grown man—all of it. It was so much easier to be Sir Galahad, unlikely knight in shining armor, riding to the rescue. Then riding on.

Except this hard, beautiful land had gotten hold of him. He liked the way sunlight fell over it, making the colors change from dull brown to gold, the way the wind blew like a thousand voices almost but not quite heard, the way a horse grew strong and proud.

The land was good, but he'd been other places that were, too, in their way. It was the woman who made the difference, who made it all come alive for him.

He'd hurt her. Nothing she could do or say to him could make him hurt as much as that realization. He couldn't stand the idea of letting her stay like that.

Whatever it cost him, he had to comfort her.

But when he got to the house, there was no sign of Annalise. The rooms were empty and barren without her. He walked back outside and looked around. Wind Dancer was missing from the paddock.

Falcon called to him. The big horse sounded worried, but that was probably just Chas's imagination. There was nothing to be worried about. Nothing at all.

Please God.

Chapter 34

The breeze was picking up as Annalise entered the canyon. Wind Dancer trod delicately along the pebble-strewn ground beside the stream. She whinnied softly, as though uncertain whether to continue.

"We might as well," Annalise said and touched her heels to the horse's sides.

Farther within the canyon, the shadows grew deeper. The temperature dropped and the air grew cooler. Annalise was just beginning to think about turning around when she stiffened suddenly. Up ahead, muted by the wind, she thought she heard voices.

Ghosts? The dead treasure hunter or the Anasazi who had tricked him? Either possibility sent a shiver of primal dread down her spine. She shook her head, exasperated at her own fear, and listened again.

There really were voices and they were coming from about midpoint in the canyon, near the spot where she and Chas had found the ledge. Silently she dismounted and crept forward on foot.

For a few moments she heard nothing and thought she might have been mistaken. But then, unmistakably, came the sound of men arguing.

"I'm telling you there's nothing to be scared of," an impatient voice said. "A child could climb that thing. Just go up and see what you find."

"If it's so easy," said another, "why don't you do it then?"

"Because I'm the boss and I call the shots, that's why. You want this job or not?"

"I'm not sure. How much you say you was paying?"

"More than enough for some bozo to climb a little cliff and see what's what. But if you won't do it, fine. How about you?"

"I don't know," said a third voice, low and wheedling. "Seems you been having a whole lot a trouble lately. Maybe this has got something to do with it. You didn't say nothing about cliffs when you hired us. We thought you was having a problem with some broad and wanted to teach her a lesson."

"This is the lesson, squat-for-brains. Now get on up there and don't give me no more lip about it. I walked more today than I have in years and it put me in a real bad mood. 'Less you boys want to find out what trouble really is, you'll do what I say.''

"Shouldn't've left the Jeep so far off," said one of the men. "Who you afraid gonna see us?"

"The buzzard that's gonna have dinner off your liver. Maybe you got all night to spend here but I sure as hell don't. Climb!"

Silence. Annalise peered from behind the rock where she was crouched. At first glance, the two men with Fuller looked like the goons who had gone after her in the parking lot.

Only when she studied them more carefully did she realize they were different men, recruits from Texas perhaps or hired on somewhere else. It didn't make much difference. They both looked mean and not overly gifted with smarts.

One spit a stream of tobacco juice and peered up at the cliff. "What you think's up there?"

"The animal your mama mated with," Fuller said. His face was bright red and sweating. He looked in about as dirty a mood as Annalise had ever seen him. "Whatta you care what's up there? Just go take a look."

"I don't like this place," the smaller of the two said. Smaller was strictly relative. He looked like he was over six feet tall and went two hundred and forty pounds easily. Fuller seemed to have a real thing for big guys with more muscle than brains.

If they wanted to climb up the ledge and take a look in the cliff room, that was fine with her. She wasn't going to hang around to see the results.

Annalise was turning to go when her foot slipped. She went down hard and only just managed to keep from crying out. It didn't help. A shower of pebbles slid down toward the stream.

"What the hell's that?" Fuller demanded.

"Somebody's here," one of the men said. "I knew we shouldn't've come, Stevie. I said it didn't look right."

"Shut up," the one called Stevie growled. "That ain't no ghost. That's a broad. Get her!"

Annalise ran, but it was no use. They were on her before she could go more than a few yards. Both needed a bath. The fetid smell almost made her gag.

"Let me go," she screamed and followed that up with a few well-aimed kicks. She'd be damned if she'd let them have it all their way. It was bad enough that she'd stupidly told Fuller about the canyon. Making it easy for them was too much.

"Bitch," Stevie groaned, grabbing at himself. The other made a lunge for Annalise. His fingers brushed her arm. Fuller was closing in from the other side, scowling fiercely and waving a gnarled walking stick in his hand.

"Stop her!" he screamed.

There was no way past them. She was cut off from reaching Wind Dancer. The one she'd kicked was straightening up again, joining the others in coming at her. She was trapped.

There was no other way to go but up.

She couldn't. What had been possible with Chas to guide and encourage her seemed utterly impossible on her own. She looked around frantically. There was no alternative. It was climb or be caught.

She climbed. Bile burned the back of her throat and she had a horrible conviction that she might be sick, but she kept going. The goons followed, with Fuller yelling encouragement from below.

Annalise didn't look down. She remembered what Chas had told her and, besides, there was no time. Whereas before they had walked slowly up the ledge, now she ran.

The men lumbered after her. She could hear their heavy breathing and sense the exaltation they felt when they believed they would quickly catch her.

Immediately above was the fissure into the rock chamber. If she went in there, she might have a chance of luring them into the passage where the long-ago searcher had died.

But the thought sickened her and there was also no guarantee it would work. She might simply find herself trapped in there with them.

But there was an alternative. The ledge continued beyond the fissure. It took her a moment to realize that for it grew narrower and looked much rougher, as though whoever had cut it had taken far less time or perhaps deliberately tried to conceal it.

She froze, certain that she couldn't go any farther. Forgetting everything she had struggled so hard to remember, she looked down. Instantly, the world whirled beneath her.

She gasped and grabbed hold of the cliff wall, struggling to hold on. Inexorably, her eyes were locked in a downward gaze. The rest of her body began to follow.

A sob broke from her. She was going to fall. At this height, there was no possibility of surviving. She would die without ever seeing Chas again, without ever having a chance to tell him that none of it—not the money or his mother or anything else he had kept from her—none of it mattered.

It was unbearable. She couldn't simply let her life end like this, not because of Fuller and his hired bears. She was a Johannsen, for heaven's sake. She had to do better.

She had to move. But her feet wouldn't obey her. No matter how she tried, she couldn't force her body away from the cliff wall she was pressed against.

She shut her eyes, whispering a prayer. The men were shouting beneath her. They had found the fissure and were distracted by it, but soon enough they would follow.

She was trapped. There was no way out and no hope of escape. It was over.

It was really and truly—

"Annalise!"

The voice, hoarse and harsh, tore through her. Her eyes shot open. Instinctively, she looked up.

"Annalise," Chas shouted. "Climb!"

She stared dumbly, unable to believe what she saw. He was there, leaning far out over the top of the cliff, the wind blowing his hair and a look of such utter determination stamped on his hard features that she was riveted by it.

So were the men below, including Fuller, who suddenly began shouting and pointing.

"Get her!" Fuller screamed. "Get her before he does!"

"Annalise," Chas called, "come on, sweetheart, you can do it. Climb up to me. I won't let you fall, I swear." He took a breath, seemed, as she had, to offer a prayer, and pleaded, "Trust me."

The wind blew harder. The men were closing on her. She felt all the fear she had ever felt—at being left alone, at losing her uncle, at having to manage by herself—all of it gathering together in a small, hard ball at the center of her being.

And she felt it crack.

"Faster!" Fuller screamed.

"You can do it, sweetheart," Chas said and held out his hand.

She climbed.

Chapter 35

"I've done dumber things," Annalise said, "but offhand, I can't think of any."

"It's all right," Chas murmured soothingly. "What counts is that you didn't get hurt."

They were in the bathroom. She was lying in the tub and he was kneeling on the mat beside her, dribbling hot water from a washcloth over the abrasions on her back. She'd most likely gotten them pressing into the wall. There were a few other cuts on her arms and hands where she'd had to grab hold of the rocks to haul herself up the last few inches before Chas could reach her. But otherwise, she was unharmed.

The same couldn't be said for Fuller and his men. The two who had come up after her had made it down most of the way all right once they realized they had no chance of catching her. But the one called Stevie had lost his balance when he was still several yards off the ground and had fallen, breaking an arm. That had led to a shouting and shoving match, with them blaming Fuller and him blaming them. It had gotten ugly.

"Billy Joe Jethro's going to rue the day he decided to do the right thing," Annalise mused as she lay back in the tub and shut her eyes. She felt blissfully relaxed, completely secure and so happy that it terrified her.

But then she was alive, and with Chas, and those two things pretty much said it all.

"It's about time he remembered what a sheriff's supposed to be," Chas said. "Fuller's broken more laws around here than anyone could list in a week. At some point, that's got to stop."

It looked like that point was now. They had him on trespassing for starters, which wasn't much but it led to a whole lot else. Stevie and his pal were so anxious to avoid any jail time on that pesky assault charge Billy Joe kept mentioning that they were talking themselves blue in the face. It seemed Fuller had hired them to—as they so delicately put it—"do a job on a lady." That added conspiracy to the tally the sheriff was keeping.

Then there was the whole business about the attack on Annalise's ranch, her truck blowing up, the assault in the parking lot. If Fuller's lawyers weren't already picking out Ivy League colleges for kids they hadn't even had yet, they were bound to be doing it soon. For sure they had stumbled onto years of very expensive litigation on Fuller's behalf. There was a chance he'd never do a day behind bars, but staying free was going to cost him the only thing he really cared about—whopping big amounts of money.

"All because he thought there were Anasazi artifacts in the canyon," Annalise murmured. "Talk about dumb. Even if he did find anything here, he wouldn't be able to sell it." She opened her eyes and looked at Chas. "Would he?"

"Sure he would. The black market for antiquities is stronger than ever. If he had found any significant artifacts, he would have made a bundle."

She sighed and leaned her head back again. The water was cooling. She'd have to think about getting out but not just yet.

"I still don't understand how he got wind of the canyon to start with."

Chas frowned. "The way I figured it, your uncle stumbled across something after the earthquake that tipped him off and he inadvertently let it slip to Fuller. But now I've got to wonder. We didn't find a trace of the Anasazi beyond the room itself and Tris couldn't have gotten up there."

Annalise hesitated. She thought back to the terror she had experienced that afternoon, the stomach-churning climb up the cliff, the overwhelming relief when she was finally caught safe in Chas's arms. It was tempting to forget everything else, but she had a responsibility—to him, to the memory of her uncle, and, too, to the spirits of the people who had come before them into this land.

"Chas?"

"Yes."

"When I was climbing up the cliff, above the room we found, I saw something else."

"What?"

"I'm not sure. It could have been a trick of light, but I think there may be another opening, higher than the one we found. It's beyond the reach of the ledge, but there's a chunk of stone sticking out in front of it. It looks as though a ladder could have spanned the distance or maybe ropes."

"Another room," he said softly. "It makes sense."

She was glad he thought so. Just then nothing made sense to her.

"No one's ever really known what happened to the Anasazi," he said, "but there are theories that another, stronger people came into this area and overwhelmed them. They may not have had much time to try to hide their greatest treasures, and they certainly knew an effort would be made to find them. It makes sense that they'd create a decoy to try to distract attention from the real hiding place."

"Then you think there may be genuine Anasazi artifacts higher up in the cliff and that the earthquake shook something loose for Tris to find?"

"It sounds like a real possibility."

They'd have to keep looking then. Somewhere in the house, in the attic or hidden away in an unnoticed box of papers, there might be a remnant of a lost civilization. But there could also be far more high up on the cliff where the wind blew endlessly.

The water was definitely cooling. She sat up, suddenly aware of her nakedness, and reached for the towel beside the tub.

Chas took it from her. Gently he put his hands under her arms and lifted her from the water. When she was standing on the mat in front of him, he slowly and methodically dried her from the top of her head to the tips of her toes.

By the time he was done, she was trembling all over. He took a fresh towel, wrapped it around her and lifted her into his arms.

"You've had a tough day. I think it's time for bed."

The sheets were soft beneath her back. Curtains blew gently at the windows. Just beyond, moonlight spilled over the land.

He sat down on the edge of the bed but made no attempt to touch her. His eyes were dark with shadows. He seemed to be waging a struggle deep within himself.

"I'm sorry," he said finally.

"For what?"

"Not telling you the truth about myself. But there is a reason. It's even a halfway good one."

"What's that?"

"I didn't realize it completely until I came back into the house and found you were gone, but for a while now I've been looking for a fresh start. There are things in my life that I really messed up and I've been trying to make right."

"You mean with Jimmy?"

"That's right. I *did* walk out on Lisa when she was pregnant with him. I'll carry the shame of that all my life, but my own childhood was grim, the money notwithstanding. I was afraid that I'd be a terrible father and I figured Jimmy would be better off without me."

"You figured wrong," Annalise said softly.

He nodded. "I know that now, but it took some time."

"Your mother—?"

"Liked to hit—a lot. She needed to control everything and she didn't care how she managed it. When she finally figured out that she couldn't control me, she went after Jimmy. I got him back and finally accepted the fact that she was a very sick woman. Where she is now, she gets the care she needs, but she'll never be able to hurt anyone again."

Annalise's throat was tight. It was so difficult for her to imagine that this proud, strong man had once been a helpless child victimized by an abusive parent. But there it was, the shadow that had lain over his spirit for far too long.

Slowly she said, "What kind of fresh start did you have in mind?"

He smiled and touched a hand to the curve of her cheek. "Well, now, I've been thinking about that. I like horses, always have, and there's something about this land. It's hard to imagine a better place to live. Then there's the fact that this place could stand some work, and I enjoy doing that."

His smile deepened. "Of course, you're not much of a cook, but that's okay. You've got other talents."

She pulled the covers up to her chin and took a swat at him. "Yeah, and I'll just bet I know what you think they are."

His eyes were suddenly serious. "You just might be wrong, unless you think of how it feels to come in from the cold to find a warm, giving woman with a proud spirit and a generous heart."

She pressed her lips together hard, determined not to cry. That had been happening too many times lately. But maybe she could be forgiven for it. After all, she'd never met a man who made her feel so intensely alive and so grateful to be that way.

"You're going to turn my head if you keep talking like that."

He laughed, a deep, rich sound that filled her with joy. "Honey," he said as he moved closer, "I plan to do a whole lot more than that."

"Chas," Annalise said a long time later.

"Hmm?"

"What would you think if we just forgot about whatever the Anasazi might have left and just let it be?"

He raised his head from where it was nestled against her breasts and looked at her. "I'd say archaeologists might miss out on a great discovery."

"I know that's a risk, but think of the excitement a future generation could have. It could be their discovery instead of ours."

In the darkness, it was hard to tell, but she thought he was smiling. "I like that."

"Leaving it for another generation?"

"Leaving it to the future." His mouth moved gently over hers. "Our future to build together."

The curtains fluttered. Annalise held him close. In the high cliffs where the wind always blew, the past lived on, waiting to be found. But in the bedroom nestled under the eaves, a man and a woman had already made the greatest discovery possible.

* * * * *

HE'S AN

AMERICAN HERO

He's a man's man, and every woman's dream. Strong, sensitive and so irresistible—he's an American Hero.

For April: KEEPER, by Patricia Gardner Evans: From the moment Cleese Starrett encountered Laurel Drew fishing in his river, he was hooked. But reeling in this lovely lady might prove harder than he thought.

For May: MICHAEL'S FATHER, by Dallas Schulze: Kel Bryan needed a housekeeper—fast. And Megan Roarke did more than fit the bill; she fit snugly into his open arms. Then she told him her news....

For June: SIMPLE GIFTS, by Kathleen Korbel: For too long Rock O'Connor had fought the good fight to no avail. Then Lee Kendall entered his jaded world, her zest for life rekindling his former passion—as well as a new one.

AMERICAN HEROES: Men who give all they've got for their country, their work—the women they love.

Only from

MILLION DOLLAR SWEEPSTAKES (III)
AND
EXTRA BONUS PRIZE DRAWING

No purchase necessary. To enter both prize offers and receive the Free Books and Surprise Gift, follow the directions published and complete and mail your "Match 3" Game Card. If not taking advantage of the book and gift offer or if the "Match 3" Game Card is missing, you may enter by hand-printing your name and address on a 3" X 5" card and mailing it (limit: one entry per envelope) via First Class Mail to: Million Dollar Sweepstakes (III) "Match 3" Game, P.O. Box 1867, Buffalo, NY 14269-1867, or Million Dollar Sweepstakes (III) "Match 3" Game, P.O. Box 609, Fort Erie, Ontario L2A 5X3. When your entry is received, you will be assigned Million Dollar Sweepstakes (III) numbers and be entered in the Extra Bonus Prize Drawing. To be eligible entries must be received no later than March 31, 1996. No liability is assumed for printing errors or lost, late or misdirected entries. Odds of winning are determined by the number of eligible entries distributed and received.

Sweepstakes open to residents of the U.S. (except Puerto Rico), Canada, Europe and Taiwan who are 18 years of age or older. All applicable laws and regulations apply. Sweepstakes offers void wherever prohibited by law. Values of all prizes are in U.S. currency. This sweepstakes is presented by Torstar Corp, its subsidiaries and affiliates, in conjunction with book, merchandise and/or product offerings. For a copy of the official rules of the Million Dollar Sweepstakes (III), send a self-addressed, stamped envelope (WA residents need not affix return postage) to: MILLION DOLLAR SWEEPSTAKES (III) Rules, P.O. Box 4573, Blair, NE 68009, USA; for a copy of the Extra Bonus Prize Drawing rules, send a self-addressed, stamped envelope (WA residents need not affix return postage) to: Extra Bonus Prize Drawing Rules, P.O. Box 4590, Blair, NE 68009, USA.

SWP-S494

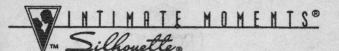

INTIMATE MOMENTS ®

™ *Silhouette* ®

continues...

Once again Rachel Lee invites readers to explore the wild Western terrain of Conard County, Wyoming, to meet the men and women whose lives unfold on the land they hold dear—and whose loves touch our hearts with their searing intensity. Join this award-winning author as she reaches the POINT OF NO RETURN, IM #566, coming to you in May.

For years, Marge Tate had safeguarded her painful secret from her husband, Nate. Then the past caught up with her in the guise of a youthful stranger, signaling an end to her silence—and perhaps the end to her fairy-tale marriage.... Look for their story, only from Silhouette Intimate Moments.

ROMANTIC TRADITIONS continues in April with
Carla Cassidy's sexy spin on the amnesia plot line
in TRY TO REMEMBER (IM #560).

"Jane Smith's" memory had vanished, so when Frank
Longford offered her a safe haven and a strong shoulder, she accepted. Then the nightmares began, with
memory proving scarier than amnesia, as Jane
began to fear losing the one man she truly loved.

As always, **ROMANTIC TRADITIONS** doesn't stop there!
July will feature Barbara Faith's DESERT MAN, which
spotlights the sheikh story line. And future months hold
more exciting twists on classic plot lines from some of
your favorite authors, so don't miss them—
only in

**And now for something
completely different
from Silhouette....**

SPELLBOUND
R O M A N C E

**In May, look for
MIRANDA'S VIKING (IM #568)
by Maggie Shayne**

Yesterday, Rolf Magnusson had been frozen
solid, his body perfectly preserved in the
glacial cave where scientist Miranda O'Shea
had discovered him. Today, the Viking warrior
sat sipping coffee in her living room, all six feet
seven inches of him hot to the touch. His heart,
however, remained as ice-cold as the rest of him
had been for nine hundred years. But Miranda
knew a very unscientific way to thaw it out....

Don't miss MIRANDA'S VIKING by
Maggie Shayne, available this May,
only from

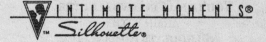

IT'S OUR 1000TH SILHOUETTE ROMANCE, AND WE'RE CELEBRATING!

JOIN US FOR A SPECIAL COLLECTION OF LOVE STORIES BY AUTHORS YOU'VE LOVED FOR YEARS, AND NEW FAVORITES YOU'VE JUST DISCOVERED. JOIN THE CELEBRATION...

April
REGAN'S PRIDE by **Diana Palmer**
MARRY ME AGAIN by **Suzanne Carey**

May
THE BEST IS YET TO BE by **Tracy Sinclair**
CAUTION: BABY AHEAD by **Marie Ferrarella**

June
THE BACHELOR PRINCE by **Debbie Macomber**
A ROGUE'S HEART by **Laurie Paige**

July
IMPROMPTU BRIDE by **Annette Broadrick**
THE FORGOTTEN HUSBAND by **Elizabeth August**

SILHOUETTE ROMANCE...VIBRANT, FUN AND EMOTIONALLY RICH! TAKE ANOTHER LOOK AT US! AND AS PART OF THE CELEBRATION, READERS CAN RECEIVE A FREE GIFT!

YOU'LL FALL IN LOVE ALL OVER
AGAIN WITH
SILHOUETTE ROMANCE!

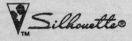

CEL1000

Three new stories celebrating motherhood and love

Birds, Bees and Babies '94

NORA ROBERTS
ANN MAJOR
DALLAS SCHULZE

A collection of three stories, all by award-winning authors, selected especially to reflect the love all families share. Silhouette's fifth annual romantic tribute to mothers is sure to touch your heart.

Available in May,
BIRDS, BEES AND BABIES 1994 is a perfect gift for yourself or a loved one to celebrate the joy of motherhood.

Available at your favorite retail outlet.

Only from

Silhouette®

—where passion lives.

BBB94

SILHOUETTE... Where Passion Lives

Don't miss these Silhouette favorites by some of our most
distinguished authors! And now, you can receive a discount by
ordering two or more titles!

D#05706	HOMETOWN MAN by Jo Ann Algermissen	$2.89 ☐
D#05795	DEREK by Leslie Davis Guccione	$2.99 ☐
D#05802	THE SEDUCER by Linda Turner	$2.99 ☐
D#05804	ESCAPADES by Cathie Linz	$2.99 ☐
IM#07478	DEEP IN THE HEART by Elley Crain	$3.39 ☐
IM#07507	STANDOFF by Lee Magner	$3.50 ☐
IM#07537	DAUGHTER OF THE DAWN by Christine Flynn	$3.50 ☐
IM#07539	A GENTLEMAN AND A SCHOLAR by Alexandra Sellers	$3.50 ☐
SE#09629	MORE THAN HE BARGAINED FOR by Carole Halston	$3.50 ☐
SE#09833	BORN INNOCENT by Christine Rimmer	$3.50 ☐
SE#09840	A LOVE LIKE ROMEO AND JULIET by Natalie Bishop	$3.50 ☐
SE#09844	RETURN ENGAGEMENT by Elizabeth Bevarly	$3.50 ☐
RS#08952	INSTANT FATHER by Lucy Gordon	$2.75 ☐
RS#08957	THE PRODIGAL HUSBAND by Pamela Dalton	$2.75 ☐
RS#08960	DARK PRINCE by Elizabeth Krueger	$2.75 ☐
RS#08972	POOR LITTLE RICH GIRL by Joan Smith	$2.75 ☐
SS#27003	STRANGER IN THE MIST by Lee Karr	$3.50 ☐
SS#27009	BREAK THE NIGHT by Anne Stuart	$3.50 ☐
SS#27016	WHAT WAITS BELOW by Jane Toombs	$3.50 ☐
SS#27020	DREAM A DEADLY DREAM by Allie Harrison	$3.50 ☐

(limited quantities available on certain titles)

	AMOUNT	$ _____
DEDUCT:	10% DISCOUNT FOR 2+ BOOKS	$ _____
	POSTAGE & HANDLING	$ _____
	($1.00 for one book, 50¢ for each additional)	
	APPLICABLE TAXES*	$ _____
	TOTAL PAYABLE	$ _____
	(check or money order—please do not send cash)	

To order, complete this form and send it, along with a check or money order
for the total above, payable to Silhouette Books, to: **In the U.S.:** 3010 Walden
Avenue, P.O. Box 9077, Buffalo, NY 14269-9077; **In Canada:** P.O. Box 636,
Fort Erie, Ontario, L2A 5X3.

Name: _____

Address: _____ City: _____

State/Prov.: _____ Zip/Postal Code: _____

*New York residents remit applicable sales taxes.
Canadian residents remit applicable GST and provincial taxes.

Silhouette®

SBACK-AJ